THE GIRL WITH THE MEMORIAL TATTOOS

THE ONE WHO HAS NOTHING TO LOSE

SHIVA KARUN GANJI

ISBN 978-93-88484-42-8

I would like to dedicate this book to the woman who went through sexual harassment and suffered from voyeurism, drug addiction and easy money.

Contents

Acknowledgements

I specially thank my senior and mentor Asma for her guidance and support all through the journey.

I thank my Relatives Nagarjuna Aitipamula and Vishweshwar Punna; Friends Kashi, Srikanth, Sanghamithra; BCF founder R.K,

Abhiram, Ravi, Sukumar, who helped me in marketing this book.

I thank my friends Tarun and Mudita who cheered and motivated me.

I thank my family for supporting me.

November, 2019

Dr. Shiva Karun

CHAPTER ONE

A TROUBLED SOUL

December 31st 2018, Night 9 PM

Bratislava - Capital of Slovaki

It was a freezing night on December 31st 2018 and the clock struck 9 PM. A terrible concoction of winds and hail stones was blowing incessantly and striking the window pane of the 2-storey Red Color house relentlessly. The snow was prevailing everywhere near few kilometers all around the house. There were few snowy mountains visible in the yonder which were identified only as vague wavy structures. Deep through the glass of the window, a hazy silhouette of a woman was visible, taking shelter before the embers emanating from the burning wood. She was handling her coffee cup with right hand and contemplating on her past incidents. Hot fumes of the coffee were rushing out from the top touching her nostrils giving a comfort feeling amidst the long-lasting winter that engulfs Slovakia every time this part of the year. But there was no comfort from the agony she was suffering from deep inside as if she was a prisoner of her mind's tricky games. The clock struck 11 PM. Malia was late to her bed being involved in solving a Rubik's cube. She was so obsessed with that game, as she found it as a refuge from the mental torment of everlasting thoughts. She looked deeply distressed with sunken eyes and dark circles beneath them. Her lips lacked smile and her face lacked glow. She was moving her hand vigorously while holding the Rubik's cube and solving it again and again. Her maid was very much concerned about her – 'Ma'am! Why are you still playing?! Please go to bed'. Malia retired to her bed mumbling something. She was lacking sleep from many nights. The reason behind it was known to very few. When everyone celebrates New Year in the end of December, she resides in her home like a coward. Only she remembers, what a terrible thing happened on the New Year just a year back. She regrets whatever happened, thinking if she could do anything better! She had a tattoo on her right hand which reminds her of the event that happened. If she hadn't been busy with getting a tattoo, she could have saved her cousin. Now, she feels dreadful on the eve of every New Year day, being frightened like a coward. For everyone, New Year is a celebration; but for her it's a mourning day. Her mother's words were still echoing in her ears, 'If you hadn't gone for a tattoo, nothing would have happened!'

She cried thinking, 'What shall I do now? I can't change the past!'

Her only memories of her dear cousin were her ashes. She made another tattoo below a previous tattoo on her right forearm; it was made out of the ink mixed with the ashes of her sister and was called a 'memorial tattoo'. It was a black tattoo in the shape of a love symbol.

December 25 2018

When she went to a bakery and ordered a cake for Christmas celebrations. She overheard a conversation between two guys who were sitting at a table ahead, while she was waiting for her order at the counter. Self-service.

'Is she the sister of that girl?'

'No dude! I am not sure'.

'She was her! See her blond hair, facial features; she looks exactly like her! See, how she is celebrating the demise of her cousin?'

And the guy opened his phone showing a video of her cousin bathing.

'I don't blame her. If I were in her position even, I would have celebrated the death of the *Bitch*' Both of them chortled into laughter.

Malia couldn't bear all that. She didn't know how to shut their mouths. She immediately wheeled towards them and strode forward. She lifted a punch upon both their faces and beat them hard with her knuckles.

'Mam. Here's your order'

The waiter shattered her imagination. She took her cake with contempt gazing at the men. The service boy reciprocated with a fake smile. She paid the bill silently, quivering with a melancholic expression, and headed out from the Bakery.

'Thank you. Please come again'.

While leaving the Bakery she could still here the giggling sound of the men. She walked away ruefully. When she could have prevented her sister from having such a terrible fate, she wasn't there, now there's nothing much she could do to shut their mouths. She had to be a victim of such criticism. She was waging a war against herself. Her brain was her enemy. She came back home and quietly occupied herself with her gaming, being involved in creating new games, finding refuge in her work.

There was a quotation lying on the wall, 'Nothing always stays the same. You don't stay happy forever, you don't stay sad forever'. Her rooms were well decorated with miniature statues of different comics and sketches. All of a sudden, her tattoo became painful and began to itch a lot, and she was mumbling incoherently with intermittent shrieks. She was wriggling with pain on her bed, when her maid came to her rescue.

December 30 2018, Morning 10 AM.

The previous day she called a Plastic Surgeon for appointment. She felt the urge to remove her tattoos. It constantly reminded her of the incident. She made an appointment with the doctor. When she was about to put the laser, Malia cried out in excessive intolerable pain. The doctor comforted her that he didn't start the procedure yet. She couldn't bear the pain and ran out of the clinic.

When she was crying in her own room, a young woman barged inside to visit her. She came close to her and soothed her. 'It's okay dear! I know what you are going through'.

Malia looked at her with sullen expression. The woman was in her near 30, fair skinned with Indian look and long black hair. Her eyes were brown and penetrating giving the woman a unique eerie appearance with a long sharp nose and high cheek bones.

'I can't bring back whom you lost but I can help you get your peace by taking revenge of the miscreants?'

'Who are you?' Malia asked with a dazed expression with the sudden appearance of this mysterious person promising her salvation.

'You will come to know who I am. For now, you can think I am a fair angel came here to guide you in the path of salvation. The more you think about me, the more you lose track on your revenge.' She put her hands over Malia, 'May I see your memorial tattoo?'

Malia held her hands, she pointed out the lower tattoo. She was fond of making memorial tattoos when someone who was endearing to her died. The upper tattoo, a replica of lower one, was a 'memorial tattoo' of her deceased father. The lady touched her hand gently and smiled at her.

'Never lose them' She handed a document to her. 'You will have complete details of the people involved in this. I was following them for the past 3 months to gather enough information for their destruction. It will help you to plan the execution of the miscreants.'

Malia said 'Thanks' with a flickering smile and a confused expression.

'No, no! I have to say thanks', said the lady hugging her and left. The next moment Malia called the doctor and cancelled her appointment for laser therapy. Her sixth sense told that her tattoos could be of aid for her. At the moment she didn't know that those mere tattoos of her can break a heart irrevocably. After the retreat of the lady she solemnly involved in her thoughts laying on her bed room. She could feel the cold crisp wind with from the window soothing her face. She sensed some comfort after so many tireless nights, with the knowledge of her targets in the document she held in her hand. She opened the documents. There was information of 4 people with their photos and the way they are linked to the death of her cousin and convincing evidence. Among them a photo of a person appalled her. She couldn't believe what she saw. She immediately threw away the file with contempt and sobbed in her tears. Again, she looked out of the window. The dark night wallowing the snowy capped mountains harbored a full moon at top. At distance she could hear howling of a wolf, hooting of an owl. In a moment the comforting ambiance felt so terrific to her. Suddenly the power cut off. She shrieked out aloud and wept into tears.

December 30 2018 Evening 4 PM

She met her psychiatrist. He checked her and comforted her that she was doing good progress. He insisted her to enter a few darker rooms with increased darkness in successive levels. When she entered into one such room, she had almost a panic attack. The doctor said, 'It's okay! You are doing good progress. Previously you couldn't come into the room'. He shifted her to level 3 which was completely a dark room, Malia had a panic attack.

December 31st at 11 PM,

That night on December 31st at 11 PM, she heard someone knocking on the door. She asked her maid to open the door. She could see the four criminals wearing masks of demons entered into Malia room and one person tried to gag her to death. one raised his axe and shoved into her stomach. She immediately kicked him in his stomach and wriggled out of their holds. She scurried into her lobby in her dark maroon Night dress. She immediately took a gun hanging over to the walls and pointed at them and killed all. She suddenly woke up from her bed and realized that was her nightmare with a happy ending. She desperately wanted that to be true. Her determination to fight became strong. She wanted revenge and made it as her New Year resolution.

CHAPTER TWO

THE FELICITATION CEREMONY

The Gandhi Medical College in Hyderabad had the beautiful Vivekananda Auditorium. Its stage was well-prepared that day. The guests took their seats in the front row. The whole auditorium was occupied by parents and family members of the students. It was not the convocation day. There was something special about the day. The students were shouting their names as they echoed through the auditorium. His parents and his younger brother were also present in the same auditorium. His father turned towards the mother and said proudly, 'Our son has made us so proud'.

The anchor, a young guy wearing a suit with well combed hair, came on to the stage. 'Ladies and gentlemen, this is the most auspicious day in the history of our college. We are proud of being with him and studying with him. Juniors feel privileged to have been ragged by him. Professors feel honored to have taken your viva.' The faculty welled up with tears! 'I am inviting our honorable the HOD of General Surgery to take the stage and present this award to him and get pardoned for all the mistakes that he has done.' The HOD came onto the stage.

Every student booed at him. The booing reverberated in the auditorium. But he kept grinning. The anchor finally announced his name. 'He is none other than Dr. Surya Aryan Seth. Surya Aryan Seth please come on the dais.' Suddenly, the revving of a Bullet motorcycle echoed through the auditorium. A young guy wearing goggles, a tight T-shirt and torn Pepe Jeans with a cigarette in his mouth, revved his bike outside. Everyone in the auditorium looked over their shoulders. The guy simply let his bike fall onto the ground near the entrance of the auditorium. As he walked into the auditorium, a spotlight focused onto him. He tilted his head to one side, brushed his beard and clenched the cigarette between his teeth. He took a deep puff and crushed the cigarette under his foot. Someone from the audience threw a Beer bottle at him, which he caught and drank in one go. He threw it back into the audience. It landed on a poor soul's head 'Someone call an ambulance!' He laughed sadistically and walked towards the stage. Everyone was looking at him with awe. He cleaned his goggles and again put them on again and tilted his head to one side with eyes looking to the roof. He stood near the stairs that led to the stage for few seconds. The HOD, who was trembling with fear, came down from the stage and felicitated Surya with a bouquet. His wife, short and stout woman, the CMO in casualty of the hospital, stood next to him. He called his daughter Shravani. She was an intern. She ran towards him and hugged him. But he didn't respond.

'Surya Sir, I didn't know you are so great! Please forgive my mistake.' said Shravani and burst into tears.

'Yes Surya!' The HOD pleaded. Surya looked at him sternly. 'Sorry Surya... *Ji*. Please forgive us'.

His wife nodded and joined him, 'Yes Surya ji. Please forgive us for our mistakes. Please marry our daughter'. Surya didn't respond. They all started falling to their knees and grabbed his legs. 'I will wash your legs with my tears'.

His father turned toward an adjacent stranger audience and started saying proudly 'That's my son', the other person reciprocated with a grin 'What an attitude! I am impressed. Wish I had a son like him.'

Everyone chanted in unison 'Surya! Surya! Surya!' Surya took his belt and began beating the trio. His mother called 'Surya!' He answered, 'wait a minute Mom' and started battering them. 'Why are you getting felicitated?'

Everyone became silent and looked with a steady grin on their faces, like idiots expecting an answer. Surya stood silent.

'Mom, I will explain it to you'.

She continued grinning, 'Surya...Surya'. Her face slowly started to contort along and her tone became harsh. The whole stage started to collapse. Surya blended into the surroundings.

'Surya! Wake up! It's getting late. Wake up Surya!'

Suddenly, Surya woke up with a flinch. 'Oh! Was that a dream?' He was annoyed at his Mom for disturbing such a beautiful dream. He was a clean-shaven and had a sharp jawline. He had brown eyes with arched eyebrows, tall with wide shoulders. His mom looked sternly at him and scolded,

'Do you know what the time is? Did you forget that you have to catch a flight to Delhi?'

Surya became alert coming out of a trance, hit his head, bulged up his eyes, and looked at his alarm clock and shrieked '9AM!'

He had a flight at 11 AM. He jumped out of bed and dashed to the sink and hastily brushed his teeth. He quickly took a shower and put on a shirt. His friends had left several missed calls. He called his friends Sudheer and Faizaan through a conference call. 'Sorry *yaar*! I woke up now. I will start in a few minutes.'

Faizaan and Sudheer stood dumbstruck. 'Hurry up Surya. What were you doing till now?'

Surya replied absentmindedly 'Dreaming' while wearing his pants. 'What?' they shouted synchronously on the phone.

'Nothing! I will come in a few minutes. What about Varsha and Rohit?' 'Idiot! I am here right now. Come fast! It's getting late', Varsha replied.

Luckily, the airport was quite close to his house. Surya took a cab and reached the Airport in less than 20 minutes. He printed his boarding pass and cleared the security check and headed towards the boarding gate. His friends were anxiously waiting for him. Varsha, who was talkative, short and had a round face, told Surya, 'Let's buy Vodka the moment when we reach Delhi'.

Surya retorted 'Stop drinking too much Varsha! You will turn into a drum and no one will marry you'. That remark irked Varsha. The rest of them laughed and high-fived each other.

Varsha's Mom made a video call. 'Sshh' Faizaan alerted.

Faizaan was tall and athletic. He put on shades for the video call. Rohit anxiously set his curly hair into order. Varsha finally answered the call and everyone said 'Hi aunty' in unison. 'So, you are the guys who are going on a holiday with my daughter!' her mother retorted.

A heated argument ensued with her mother. 'Varsha! Whom did you inform before planning all this? Once you come back home, I am going to punish you. I'll see to it that you get as soon as possible. This is absolutely unacceptable'

'Mom! I am just 23! Why marriage?' she shrieked much to the annoyance of their co-passengers. She abruptly ended the call when the final announcement for boarding the aircraft was made.

'Sorry guys! My mother can be so difficult to deal with at times.'

'No *yaar*! She is your mother. She is Adolf Hitler's twin sister', Surya teased. Everyone chortled into laughter.

Varsha gave a grim expression. They adjusted in their respective seats and the flight took off to Delhi.

CHAPTER THREE

BEGINNING OF A BRIGHT DAY

Surya got out of bed with a spirit of cheerfulness lingering in his eyes. On most days he'd wake up with an expressionless face and groan when he'd imagine the boring day that lay ahead of him. Today was a special day – first day of the vacation in Manali. He had booked a room in the Folklore hostel along with his friends two days ago. He hadn't appreciated the beauty of the room when he'd checked in at night. But in the presence of early morning sun he could see the room colorfully occupied with bunk beds on either side of the window. His friends were sleeping tight. Bharat was hugging his pillow and his lips were in a pout. 'Idiot!' remarked Surya looking at Bharat's face. 'Get up! Bharat! You were the one who planned everything. You have to take the lead. Instead, you are kissing your pillow!' Bharat lazily opened his eyes, gave an idiotic smile and replied, 'Even pillows need a boyfriend *yaar*' and chuckled at his lame joke!

Surya sighed and though about the helpless situation he was in. He washed his face in the sink and stood in the balcony. He was eager to the beautiful city. He stared at the two-storied wooden cabin with a sloping roof.

Chakradhar greeted him 'Good Morning Surya! Oh Man you look like you did push-ups just now! You look like a bodybuilder man!'.

Surya had worn a full sleeve T-shirt in the last two days and nobody had noticed his arms until then. Anyhow, Surya was not in the mood for any small talk. He wanted to explore the hidden beauty of the city. exploring the hidden beauty of Manali. A few moments later Neha appeared in the adjacent balcony. She waved at Surya and took a deep breath in the pine-scented air. She'd let down her long wavy hair. She looked beautiful in the early morning sun. 'This air definitely has some magic', she said looking over her shoulder with a pretty smile. Her cheeks looked flushed. Surya seconded her saying 'Yeah exactly! The air you are breathing'. She chuckled, 'Come on! Don't flirt so early!'.

She chuckled and then and turned to the balcony and continued sipping her coffee. Then he heard the creaking sound of a door disturbing his focus. It was a tall lean spectacled woman with boy-cut hair, Kiran aka Kiranmayi. People call her Kiran as she acted like a tomboy. She greeted them. Surya halfheartedly welcomed her. Kiran stood next to Surya with her back aligning with the railing of the balcony. 'I didn't know you are a good dancer Surya', Surya looked puzzled.

'Don't you remember what happened yesterday? You were dancing all over the floor after getting too drunk'. Surya felt shocked. Neha gave a surprising look. In the meantime, Bharat joined the trio.

Bharat was slightly dark complexioned and had a funny looking face. With his eloquence, he could mingle with any group and disturb anyone's peace of mind with his sarcastic comments. Surya thought, 'Oh God! Planets are planning against me. With the coming of this Saturn, Venus wouldn't stay for long', casting a quick glance towards Neha.

'You don't know about Surya! He has done many extraordinary things after getting drunk. Once, he just gave his bike keys to a complete stranger!'. Surya turned red with embarrassment. Neha and Kiran were laughing. Bharat continued, 'The next day he was messaging in the group and enquiring about his bike. Finally, the guy replied and gave his bike that afternoon'. Neha and Kiran chuckled at Surya. Neha started teasing, 'Hey Hero! Why were you so desperate to get your bike back? Planned any movie with your girlfriend?' and continued laughing. Kiran remarked, 'OMG! I used to think I was so spoiled. This is the first time that I am seeing someone who is more spoiled than me', not knowing whether she made fun of Surya or herself.

Surya tried to salvage the last bits of his respect, took a deep breath and said, 'I truly trusted that guy! You know I can look at someone's face and tell what kind of a person they are even if I am drunk. My judgement wasn't wrong. He returned my bike the next day', and then he faked a confident smile, checking others' faces to see if his trick worked. Kiran, Bharat and Neha burst into laughter. Surya frowned as they laughed. Neha tried to control her laughter but she again burst into laughter. Surya turned away with an angry look and went downstairs for a walk on the streets. He could still hear their laughter from a distance.

CHAPTER FOUR

LIVE IN RELATIONSHIP

Life is vicissitude. It's your choice that decides whether you go immaculate or sordid'. These lines echoed in Surya's head while he was going downstairs, introspecting the events that had happened the day before. Chakradhar, Bharat, Surya and Kiran were sitting on the 2nd floor of the wooden cabin opposite to the Folklore Hostel. Surya ordered a beer for himself while Kiran ordered Vodka for herself. She missed her kids but was still feeling relieved at being away from her mother-in-law. She gulped the shot in one go and munched on the Paneer tikka. Chakradhar was a tall, middle-aged man, with a bass voice that didn't go well with his melancholic face most of the times. He kept to himself while he drank beer and smoked a cigarette, indiscreetly mumbling about his 'cursed' life. It wasn't clear if he was cursing his own life or wife, he was glad to be away from his wife. They knew very little about him as he was an introvert. Even Surya had a feeling of freedom being away from his Mom. It seemed like as if everyone had some rivalry with a woman. Even a woman is an enemy to another woman. Surya always felt that women should be considered as a different species.

Chakradhar sat beside Surya and was ready to begin a monologue about his family, wife and children.

'You know Surya? Marriage is a quagmire. Once you get into it, it's not easy to come out. You wriggle all the way just to know that you have been sufficiently buried. Yeah, marriage is like a black hole. It sucks a man's entire life'. He gulped his beer. Kiran was listening keenly, swaying occasionally, but maintaining her disposition. 'So Chakradhar babaji, what do you suggest instead of getting married, *Babaji ka thullu?'* and chortled into laughter.

'Live-in relationship!' Chakradhar took one more gulp experiencing his sense of elation. 'It is the solution to all your problems. Check compatibility before you commit and breakup if you don't like'.

Kiran sat before him like a disciple, 'Like a product on Amazon'.

'Exactly', Chakradhar continued with his sermon. Surya was observing them keenly. 'You know, Sri Krishna and Radha never got married. But their love was eternal'.

Kiran added, 'If Shah Jahan and Mumtaz were in a live-in relationship, Shah Jahan would have never built the Taj Mahal'.

Surya raised his voice for the first time in a while, 'Kiran! Taj Mahal was a symbol of true love, not his marriage', and he winked at Chakradhar. Chakradhar slowly lied down on one side with the support of an elbow, and palm placed beneath his head, taking the posture of Lord Vishnu, 'Yes! If I had the clarity you had at that time, I would have been much happier', he said and started singing a song 'don't marry be happy' in a low melancholic tone, with his thick voice crescendoing and later his tone hushed gradually as he dozed off to sleep. Kiran turned pale as the only source of entertainment was gone. She glanced at Surya who in turn shrugged his shoulders and stood up from his place fearing that he would have to listen to another sermon, this time from Kiran.

Then the live concert of the foreigners started. They were probably performing Spanish songs. Surya peeked over the balcony to see what was happening. A foreigner with long hair, thick beard and moustache, and a tattoo on left arm, was playing his guitar on the stage. A beautiful girl, probably in her mid-twenties was dancing rhythmically to the music. She was fair, with black hair and black eyes. Faizaan, one of Surya's friends from Hyderabad, joined the show dancing. He danced rhythmically to the music with an enchanting smile as if he had a master plan to impress the girl. Surya felt an awkward feeling as he was probably jealous. Surya had planned this trek of Hampta pass with a few of friends.

Unfortunately, one of their friends got injured while trekking, so Faizaan took the responsibility of taking him back to the base camp and then to Manali. He hadn't heard from Faizaan since then.

Faizaan stayed back in Manali while the other guys left for Hyderabad. He was a fitness freak. When Surya, Faizaan, Varsha and Rohit landed in Delhi airport the first thing they did was buy a bottle of Vodka. At the base camp of Hampta pass, the rest of them consumed the Vodka to overcome the chill that night without telling Surya. He was annoyed that he could not join in the drinking party. When Faizaan and his friends celebrated that night drinking Vodka, Surya had to keep dreaming about the plan to drink the Vodka in some other tent. The worst thing was that Surya continued believing that the Vodka was still sealed. Only when Faizaan was leaving with his injured friend Rohit, he whispered told Surya about the mini betrayal. It was too late by then as Faizaan was leaving for Hyderabad. Surya knew little about his stay in Manali. He never thought he would get his chance for revenge.

Surya climbed down the stairs and stood beside the stage. He wanted to join the dance while the other part was scared. Surya was completely dependent on his beer bottle for boosting him. He was taking a sip and trying to step forward but didn't feel confident enough. So, he stepped back and had another sip. Kiran was watching him and giggling. He finished a bottle of beer but still there was no sign of hope. Surya went upstairs, consumed s another beer and then he slowly advanced toward the dance floor. Many foreigners had joined by then. He began dancing to the music more than enough to enjoy the music less enough to be spotted. But one foreign girl spotted him and welcomed him to join the dance floor.

Surya felt like his dream came true. With a vivid sense of confidence, he stepped right into the dance floor and started copying the steps of whoever he had seen. Sometimes he even tried to invent his own steps. Somehow, he seemed to enjoy the music. He forgot the world. All he remembered then was the beautiful Spanish music and the bottle of Beer he left on the table. At that moment he saw his friend cum enemy Faizaan. Suddenly, a flush of anger flew through his veins. He felt like it was the right moment. He sneaked behind Faizaan and tried to trip him with his leg. Bang! Faizaan fell on the floor breaking his nose. Another person stepped on his hand and he cried out in pain. The security guards arrived and took him out. Surya enjoyed all this with a sadistic happiness. '*My precious Vodka*' – Surya grinned as he thought of Gollum from *The Lord of the Rings*.

Now it was only music, dance and beer mattered to him. The alcohol induced euphoria gave him a heightened freedom and happiness. He danced to his heart's content and left the dance floor after feeling completely exhausted. It was around 11PM. He took a narrow lane adjacent to the *Old Manali*. The signboards of the bars and restaurants were glittering. The uphill road was narrow and occupied by pedestrians who were shopping in Manali. He passed Kiran, Chakradhar and Bharat. They were headed downhill to the *Pink Panther*. Surya strode along the path, dodging the oncoming vehicles and entered a restaurant called *Over the Moon*. Some of his friends were already sitting there. Neha was also present. She sat beside Nazma, a chubby short girl in her black dress. Neha and Nazma were childhood friends. Nazma had moved to Manali after completing her education.

Surya sat beside Sudheer. He was a lean and wore spectacles. He had an innocent face and was always well-mannered. He'd knew him since his school days. Surya had a great bond with him.

There was live music in the restaurant too. The band was taking song requests. The melody of the songs suddenly changed to a romantic Song. Surya couldn't help himself but cast his eyes over Neha. She looked like a diva. He could see her eyes dancing to the music, her lips humming to the melody. He felt that he should ask her out on a date. Neha was from Rajasthan. She came from a traditional Jain family. Very little was known about her. Suddenly a Muslim friend of Neha, her office colleague, passed some rotis to Surya across the table. Surya couldn't deny her offer so he accepted the rotis. He was cherishing the delicacy while staring at Neha!

'So, Neha, what's your opinion about live-in relationships?'

Nazma and Sudheer stopped their activities and stared at Surya. Neha being from an orthodox family was expected to debate against it.

'A live-in relationship? I think it's a good idea'. Everyone was shocked by her answer. Nazma interfered, 'How can you bluntly say that? Live-in relationship is not a part of Indian culture'.

'What's wrong in that? Don't we order some product on Flipkart, and return it if we don't like it?'

'How can you compare a marriage with a stupid Amazon product?' Sudheer corrected 'Flipkart!'

Nazma cried, 'Whatever Dumbo! Flipkart or Amazon',

'Even in mythology, Sri Krishna never married Rukmini', Neha retorted. Surya corrected, 'Radha you mean?'

'Oh yeah Radha! Was he not happy?' Neha exploded.

Sudheer and Surya were enjoying the heated argument. 'Why don't you think about Lord Rama?'

'Whatever! If my parents had tried a live-in relationship before marriage, I wouldn't have watched all that domestic violence in my childhood. Now my Mom is living with my father just for my sake', said Neha with a strained voice.

'I am extremely sorry Neha for raising that topic', Surya said apologetically. 'Even I am Sorry Neha!' Nazma apologized. 'It's okay guys! Chill! I just told... being out of control', Neha faltered.

Nazma laid her hands over her shoulder. Neha suddenly burst into tears and hugged her. Surya assumed there a lot of intensity deep within those superficial smiles. Everyone has a tragedy. Some people end up in depression, some turn into monsters while some seek to escape them in the company of their friends. One can share anything with a good friend. Surya pondered over the beauty of friendship.

'Tell me Neha! Do you have a boyfriend?' Surya asked with a cunning smile to ease the air. 'Why? Do you want to be in live-in relationship... with my boyfriend?'

Everyone burst into laughter.

Nazma wished everyone goodnight and left. Pondering about all that happened in Over the Moon Restaurant the day before, Surya was stepping down the stairs. He felt a tinge of romantic feeling as he recalled Neha's laugh. Though those guys made fun of him, Neha's smile was all that he could remember. He wished he could confidently express his feelings to Neha.

CHAPTER FIVE

THE RUSSIAN GIRL

Bharat, Sudheer and Surya planned to go for shopping. Manali is famous for its Jerkins. The quality of the leather is so good. The trio went inside a Leather shop.

The shopkeeper greeted them, 'Aayiye Saab! What are you looking for?'

Bharat replied, 'Bhai! We are looking for Jerkins could you show me a few.'

The shopkeeper showed a few jerkins. Bharat tried a jerkin. When he looked into the mirror, his paunch was pressing upon the buttons with a pressure which Virat Kohli exerts on his bat. Bharat suddenly removed the Jerkin, pretended nothing happened, to overcome the embarrassment. Surya gave it a try. It looked very well on his fit body.

The shop owner appreciated, 'Masth hai Bhai! It's looking perfect on you'. Surya wondered if it's a genuine comment or a trick played by shop owners to attract their customers to purchase their products. Bharat was trying the outfits one after another. Nothing seemed satisfactory for him. Surya chuckled at the helpless situation of Bharat and made funny comment, 'I will get you a membership in Gym. Come here a year later after reducing your paunch'.

Bharat looked serious. Sudheer was trying an outfit. He asked the owner 'Bhai! What is its price?'

It was a chocolate colored leather jerkin which was looking good on him. The shop owner replied, 'It's actually 2,500 but you look like a gentleman and came from far away. So, I can give you discount on this. You can take it for 2000'.

Sudheer felt so happy! Bharat took him aside and whispered something. They were talking to each other as Team India was planning to win over its opponent in cricket.

Bharat took the lead and asked the owner, 'I have a number in my Mind. Tell me if it is possible to give at that price'.

Shop owner asked 'Tell bhai! What's the price you want for?' Bharat slowly bent over the desk and cautiously said, 'We will give you 500'.

The owner impatiently asked them, 'Get out of my shop quickly before I throw you douchebags out'.

Surya got shocked. He didn't expect Bharat would stoop so low to ask for such a low price and Shopkeeper would react in such a harsh way. Immediately they ran out of Shop!

On the way, Bharat was talking to Sudheer laying his hand over his shoulder, walking ahead of Surya. 'Come on yaar! Let's find another shop. We can find such jerkins so cheaply. This Shopkeeper is trying to fool us'.

Sudheer nodded his head like a sheep, 'Yeah exactly! Let's try in some other shop. We will definitely find a better one for better price'.

By this time Surya lost his patience. He cursed Bharat that he couldn't buy the jerkin he liked because of his stupid bargaining. 'It's not stupid, it's bizarre to ask such way', he shouted angrily at Bharat. 'Come on Surya! Let's find a better one', Bharat replied frivolously.

'You guys just go ahead; I am tired of this Shopping'.

Bharat shrugged his shoulders 'Yeah it's ok! Sudheer, let's finish our hunt'.

Surya retreated on his path to reach his Hostel. On the way there was a Burger shop in which the Russian girl who had danced before, was sitting silently and having burger. He remembered the time with her.

After the dance, the Russian girl and her guitarist friend, who too was a Russian, were enjoying their dinner. After their performance, they threw a party for themselves. Surya felt inspired from their performance. He wanted to appreciate them. He himself was a guitarist so it's natural for him to be curious about the couple. Moreover, he was infatuated for the foreign girl. When he was about to greet them, to his surprise, Faizaan already took his seat facing them. Surya approached the guys. Faizaan with his mischievous eyes remarked, 'What a dance Surya!' Surya nodded and smiled with suspicion if Faizaan came to know that he was the one who made him slip. Half-heartedly he shook hands with Faizaan who was soothing his nose with ice. Surya with a pretended shock asked, 'What happened Bhai? You look like injured'.

Faizaan appreciated his concern, 'It's okay bhai! Just an accident'.

'Accident! Shall I call an ambulance?' Surya taunted wickedly.

'Thanks, yaar! I am fine! Don't do too much melodrama now'

Surya smiled with a cunning face and sat down with those guys. He looked at the Russian girl 'Whoa! What a dance! What a guitar performance! Mind-blowing yaar'.

The Russian girl replied 'Thank you' with a smile glowing on her face. 'Even we appreciate you guys' performance. Thanks for encouraging us'.

'Manali will take care of guys who have talent. So, what was the dance style?'

'It's just mixed Russian dance, had no name for that'.

'OH, I see! Just like our Bollywood dance! We mix different varieties of dance', he said with the air of connoisseurship.

Then the Russian guitarist began lighting a cigarette while meticulously handling it from his packet. Surya doubted if it was Charas 'weed' which was so famous in Manali. Surya wanted to try once. He had never tried cigarette before but had a desire of trying weed. He observed the Russian who lit his lighter and started warming the cigarette which was in his mouth, all through length of the cigarette before lightening it. Surya looked puzzled why he was doing that.

He asked straightly, 'Why do you do that?' The guitarist looked at an angle with raised eyebrow and a cigarette in his mouth, being unable to understand what he meant. Surya clarified 'I mean you warmed the cigarette, what is it for?'

The guitarist explained, 'Yeah it is to dry the Cigarette so that it gives more pleasure later'.

The female Russian interrupted, 'Well that is Charas! If you have any disputes with your friends, it calms down' winked toward Surya. He looked puzzled.

Faizaan bid bye to everyone 'Chalo guys! Catch up later!' still holding ice pack which melt to water by then. Even the guitarist went away being exhausted with his performance. Surya hesitated to ask but mustered his courage and asked suspiciously, 'What was that about?'

The Russian girl put her elbows on the table, moving a little closer to him and whispered 'Well, I saw you!'

'Huh?'

'Yeah I saw you how you tricked him to fall accidentally', she winked at him.

Surya shocked. 'You saw?'

'Well you think I only care about music and dance? So, what was all that?'

'Well it's a big story. Simply a Vodka dispute'.

'It seems like you guys are on uneven terms tonight; dispute by vodka should be settled with Charas'.

'I will buy some then. Seems like you are selling some and it's a salesman's trick' Surya shrugged.

'Whatever you think' She stood up with a smile and was about to leave.

'You didn't say your name!' Surya asked.

'Well, you people couldn't even pronounce our names. Why do you struggle to remember me?'

'I don't think it's much of struggle to remember your name. After all, our mind remembers the things which are only interesting, beautiful... umm'.

'Okay, okay, enough! I understand you are in a mood to flirt' the girl looked at him with her eyes wide opened, pretending anger. 'Seriously! You don't want to remember me when you know more about me'.

Surya couldn't understand what she meant. He looked down only to see her feet just to confirm if she was real or ghost. When he looked down under the table in the pretext of taking the Beer bottle he put on the floor, he couldn't see the feet. He was frightened. He checked above the table. To his shock he couldn't see the girl too. She was leaving away waving goodbye to him. 'By the way, my name is Andria!'

Today he saw Andria in Bakery. She ordered Chocolate brownie! She was waiting for her order. Her face was calm, carefree as if she had all the time on Earth to wait. She was listening to music while humming to the songs. Surya took a chair opposite her swiftly and greeted her,

She reciprocated with a cute smile. Surya felt something in that smile. He ordered 'Death by chocolate'. She faced her phone selecting the track list.

Surya teased, 'Well it's better to die of Chocolate than being in suspense about a girl'.

The girl chuckled, 'Better die drowning in the chocolate then' and was still fixed on her phone.

There was a quotation on the wall. 'If the world is Being, hypocrisy is its Disposition. Don't worry about it, just beware of it'.

Surya was pondering upon the quotation. Andria waved her hand over his face. 'What are you looking at?'

'I think about my life'. Surya continued staring deeply at the quotation, 'I wanted to be a writer but I sacked up into this medical Profession'.

'I wanted to be a doctor and right now doing concerts.' Andria said with a cunning look.

'Concerts... good right? New songs, new people, lot of encouragement?' Surya widened his eyes.

'We always feel jealous about others' lives and feel low about ourselves. You didn't see much world'. She stood right there at her place hanging her hand bag over shoulders, paid the bill for the Brownie she ordered before and waved at Surya.

'Let's go! Before you end up thinking to become a chef' She joked.

'Where?'

'See for yourself' She shrugged.

'death by chocolate?!'

She pulled him dragging his hands and pushed him forward.

Andria drove him on her Activa bike. The cool morning wind was blowing against his face. Surya asked aloud,

She pulled the vehicle over a market place. The place was crowded with vendors on each side. Surpassing the market there was an open space full of sand, looked like a beach.

After reaching the shore she showed the sea, 'turbulent outside but deep inside it has its true nature. Peaceful and giving shelter to beautiful creatures.'

Surya sighed. 'You brought here to show me the beach?! I watch it every day in National Geography channel. If you asked me, I could have showed you there at home in TV' He chuckled and looked leisurely towards her. She folded her hands with a serious look. He shut his mouth to let her say.

'When I look deep in your eyes, I can see what you are going through.' she wheeled towards him. Her long hair blew over her face. She carefully brushed away her hair tendrils. 'I can see deep inside you through your eyes behind the fake smile. Everyone does have problems and running away is not always the solution.' Surya was quite an introvert. Expressing his problems to another person seems ridiculous and bothering for him. He was taken aback with her statement and left perplexed.

To his relief, a vendor selling cotton candy approached them.

Andria gave a break to her monologue to ease the tension and gazed at the cotton candy. 'This reminds my childhood memories of buying candy on roadside.' Surya smiled.

'It's worth to rejoice them again' She looked at the candy vendor, a middle-aged man with a turban over his face and tanned skin with curled moustache wearing shabby clothes. 'How much is the cotton candy?'

He perplexed. Surya explained him properly in the local language.

'20 rupees. Sir'.

'Why are you looking at my face? Give him money'.

Surya became wary all of a sudden as if someone poured filtered hot coffee on his face, and gave money to the vendor. Andria was walking step by step on sand which was showing imprints of foot behind her. Surya followed her, tracing her footsteps in silence, appreciating the sea, the winds, the wet sand and the whole ambiance occupied by the chattering of the tourists of varied age, a mother caring for her toddler son. An old father being cared by his son. A young couple making plans for their future. Different phases of an entire life cycle of human being were wandering around him.

'Human relations are weird. Why would be someone so happy seeing the same face all the time. I feel bored by meeting the same friend again' Surya broke the silence.

'Sometimes you can feel the value of a person only when you lose them. Until then these relationships seem like an act in circus to impress someone' She said curtly.

'You talk older than your age with maturity, being carefree as you have all the time in this world and no problems?'

'I do bother about problems but I prefer to look at the positive side. I have ecstasy in living this way. It wasn't this way before. I had a terrible tragedy. I was depressed and lived like dead. Time heals. Need to move on'.

'Sounds like a love failure. Happens. Glad that you moved on'.

'Perspective. Spend time with friends, develop hobbies which you love to do, live like there is no tomorrow. See how you don't move on. Don't expect any angel would knock your door someday with the solution for all your problems'.

Surya chuckled. 'Angels? I don't believe in God, forget about angels.' Surya pondered upon something deeply. 'When you told about hobbies, I recalled the way James plays his guitar. How did he become so good at it?'

'Everyone does have their own part of struggles. James was a drug addict some time ago. He is my step brother. My father had a love affair before his marriage. That person was frivolous minded, irresponsible. James had a problematic family all his childhood. His mother abused him. When my father came to know about that, he tried to change her behavior and make her a better person but he couldn't succeed. One fine day he divorced her, admitted in asylum and married my mother. James was irrevocably damaged by then. He had bad friendship and got addicted to the drugs. We tried to get him out of that habit. Old habits die hard. When I realized his passion on guitar, it was easy for our family to encourage him to focus on guitar after his rehab program.'

'Sounds like an inspiring story.' Surya commented.

'You will feel that ecstasy even in your life if you focus on what you are passionate about. Many people get lost in the flow following a herd. Instead, it's better you make your own way and struggle to know who you are. It shows how beautiful your life is. Just use that confidence upon other skills. Focus one at a time', she told that while eating her cotton candy.

'I want to write a Novel'. Surya remembered his passion.

'Good. I am going to see you as an author in near future', Andria said with a glow in her eyes. It was relaxing for Surya to look into her eyes and her smile. It was more beautiful than anything else in this world.

'But there is no support from my family. I even felt so ashamed of myself to say that I want to be a writer.' Surya said apologetically.

'What do you have to be ashamed about?' she asked with a gentle smile.

'I don't know. I feel so worried about how people judge me. Sometimes I fear that what if I end up in writer's block and just can't come out through it... what...', Surya faltered.

'Surya! Just come out of your fear. Nothing great can be achieved without being scared initially. It's okay to have fear but don't let it conjure you. Whatever fears you are facing now were faced by someone at some time. It's not just you.' Andria shrugged. 'Just see such exemplary persons. Know about how they succeeded in it.

Inspire from their lives. You will always have an answer. Don't think too much about what the world thinks. Follow your passion, success will followyou'. Andria ended her speech.

A small kid was passing by, playing with a kite. It's so beautiful to see his smile, being carefree not thinking about anything. Andria showed the kid. 'What is he so worried about in this world! Everyone had been a kid once. We never felt so crumbled up with our thoughts then. Wake up the child within you, he will wake up new world within you'.

Surya was experiencing an epiphany in her presence listening to whatever she was saying. Hypnotizing.

'When I was a writer, I had to face some difficulties. There was no support from my parents too', Surya told with an effect of melancholy.

'Remember a shark in a fish tank will grow 8 inches but in an ocean 8 feet or more. Shark will never outgrow its environment. Same way human beings too. You are outgrowing yourself. Don't think everyone will support you and praise you. Be prepared for criticism. At the same time work hard to achieve praise...'.

Her words felt assuring for Surya. 'I am good at writing; I enjoy it but I am bad at marketing. It's so stressful' he told with a strain in his voice.'

'One day you will become famous for your books' Said while munching the cotton candy. 'Where there is a will, there's a way. Be positive. You know what's the quality of a good writer? He doesn't just write what he sees, but expresses along with what he feels. It's not just about inspection, but something deeper, inspiration'.

There was silence for some time. Andria broke the silence.

Surya and Andria were walking ahead. The beach was pleasant with the beautiful sound of sea with its tides touching the shore like a mother caressing her child.

'Shall we go near the sea?'

'Do you want to drench in water?' Surya trembled even with the mere thought.

Surya had fear of water. Superstitious. The Swamiji, who his father

was a disciple of, inculcated this fear that he had threat from water.
'Andria! I have life threat with water'.
'Did you stop bathing then?' She laughed heaving her bosom heavily. She nudged him to go near the shore. Surya felt a chill passing through his body when a low tide of water touched his feet. He started shivering initially but slowly felt comfortable with it.
'How do you feel now?' Andria asked with a smile throwing her hair across her face which was dancing to the wind.
'It's good'. A smile flickered over the lips of Surya. 'I can feel the sand underneath my feet slipping off'.
'Doesn't it feel amazing.', she told whimsically. 'Let's go nearer.'
Surya contemplated for a moment, took a deep breath, gathered all his courage and went deep into the water making small strides along with Andria in perfect synchronicity. Andria grabbed Surya's right hand with her left hand gently, which passed goosebumps in him. He appreciated that her hands were soft and cool with tender fingers, emerging from the palm as the branches of a holy tree. She entwined her fingers with his.
'Sit!' He was in some kind of trance state being completely hypnotized by her enchanting words. He was ready to jump into the sea at her will. They took a seat on the wet sand relaxedly with water touching his bottom, which made Surya feel some current passing through him.
'Look at that! Tide is coming!' He looked suddenly when Andria grabbed his back. He slowly slipped his hands hesitantly over her back while Andria was looking at the tide with a beautiful smile on her face, with fibrils of hair covering her eyes which she gently brushed aside. 'Be alert, the tide is coming!'
And she grabbed him tightly. He also grabbed her closely feeling bosom heaving against his body with her respiration. The tide hit them and went past. Both of them lifted slightly with the force of water and came back to position again, feeling the sand slipping beneath their bottom.
'We have been for a long time'. Andria said relaxedly being content.
'We can stay a bit longer' Surya mused.

'I heard someone saying that he had a life threat with water'. Andria teased him playfully.
They were walking on the beach with wet clothes, enjoying the weather. It's already evening.
Surya just lost track of time in her presence. Andria nudged him, which made him to be alert. She showed an old woman selling globe-shaped glass inside which there was a beautiful model of Taj Mahal with sprinkles spread all around in Brownian motion.
'It's so beautiful. I like it'.
Surya looked into the woman's eyes and asked her the price.
She told it's 50 rupees. Surya had 100 rupees and gave it to her. She was about to give 50 change but something in him stopped to take it.
'It's ok. Just keep the change'.
The old woman smiled pleasantly exposing her sparsely toothed gums. Surya reciprocated with gentle smile. They were heading out of the beach where he surpassed a man with his son straddled over his neck. Surya was observing them. It reminded of his childhood memories when he was happy with his father. As time passed, distance began growing between them.
Andria interrupted him with gentle tender voice asking, 'Do you remember, he was the man from whom you bought cotton candy?'
He looked again keenly over his shoulder. 'You saw the cotton candy earlier, now you are seeing how your money gave happiness to them'.
The father made some candy and gave it to his 5-year-old son 'How was it...?' the kid nodded his head with appreciation of the delicacy.

A carefree haughty smile blossomed on Surya's lips.
He turned toward Andria and asked. 'Even the old woman was so happy with the little she was earning.'
'Money is not everything', Andria said with a pleasant smile. 'Your money gave value to their lives. If you see the same with your profession, you feel good'. Her words had an effect on him. He looked Andria out of gratitude and hugged her. Gently caressed her

hair.

'Thank you'.

She patted his shoulder gently.

An old man walking beside the beach, with his dog seeing strangely at Surya! It seemed like the dog sensed something, as if dogs can sense catastrophes earlier than humans. It barked loudly. The old man held the dog in control and left the place. Surya couldn't take off his eyes on the dog. And the real quake was yet to begin. Surya waved bye to Andria, who later went to visit her friend and Surya left for his hostel

CHAPTER SIX

ANYTHING FOR OUTFIT

When he was walking down the lane toward his Folklore hostel, recapitulating the events happened with Andria, serenely. He got a call from Faizaan! 'Bhai! I am going to show you Manali's special... be there in the room by evening'.

'What's the special?'

'Surprise man! Get the child in you get more curious. What I will show you will just change your life'.

'Man, you talk too much. Let's see'.

Surya wondered whether it was any tactic to take revenge on him. Anyhow it didn't matter. Faizaan never had brains to find out what exactly happened that night of concert. He would never know unless someone says.

'What if Andria said anything? Why would she meddle with us?'

'Is that any birthday surprise what Faizaan was talking about? Whose birthday is it today in our team?' So many thoughts started rolling in his head. He thought 'let's wait and see.'

As he was passing, pondering about Faizaan, soon he had seen a theatre like structure on his way. It's not a theatre but by closely observing he realized it's a circus. Posters on the walls were so intriguing. An old guy with his weird costume was standing among beautiful girls bedazzling with shiny costumes on either side. Some posters were showing him while he was doing some magic. Another poster was a clown riding a unicycle. His nose was holding a red bulb. It resembled to Faizaan's face the day he fell down on his nose. His nose bruised a lot and appeared like a clown. But he still suspected something devilish about him. It looked like a clown in the movie IT. Faizaan had some dark self being hidden from people. 'I will find that', Surya jumped up with an exaggerated excitement to challenge him.

He soon reached his hostel. It was noon by then. Surya went to his room and occupied the lower bed on the left side of the window. He saw there was a charging point with 2 plug sockets. Bharat put his phone on charging. He tried the socket beside it to charge his phone.

Unfortunately, it didn't work. So, he removed Bharat's phone and put his camera for charging. Little he knew that Bharat was on his way to the room. He heard the creaking sound of the door. He saw Bharat entered into room. Bharat saw Surya rather with a studying face and observed that his phone was removed. Bharat with controlled anger demanded, 'Why you removed it?'

'I need to charge my camera man!'

'Why didn't you try other socket?'

'It's not working dude'.

Bharat impatiently tossed over the bed to take his phone with charger and put the charger into the socket and turned on the switch. Surya was shocked as it started charging. He put a blank face not knowing how to explain that. He helplessly looked at Bharat and gave a grin. Bharat just tossed his head to the other side rather angrily, stood up and left the room, shut the door with a loud thud.

Surya immediately followed Bharat to pacify him. 'Come on ya! Just chill. Why was I so eager to charge my Camera?'

'Why?'

'So that I can take good snaps of you'.

It made Bharat curious. 'Acha!'

Kiran was passing that way then. She was curious about their conversation and stopped to eavesdrop on them.

'Yeah! I heard that you were not getting good matches. These pictures can help you woo girls'. Bharat became melodramatic. 'You are a real friend. See Kiran, this is what true friendship is. Learn from him'.

Kiran was taken aback with this sudden remark from Bharat.
Surya continued, 'Yeah! There is no mountain you didn't climb, and no god you didn't pray for a girl. At least, if you get a girl, you will get rid of this overwhelming burden of climbing mountains and we will get rid of overly sarcastic douchebag like you'. Surya laughed.
Bharat took time to understand the meaning of his monologue, turned his face into anger. Suddenly Kiran burst into laughter saying, 'Crazy! Yours Tom and Jerry fighting started again huh?' In the meantime, Surya escaped into his room and locked it.
Bharat banged the door, 'Open the door Man!' Surya was chuckling on the other side of the door.
After some time Sudheer knocked on the door. 'Come on Man! Open the door', Surya was listening to some songs in his mobile while enjoying the view from his window sill. Suddenly, he heard the banging of the door and opened the door. Sudheer angrily asked 'Why it took so much time?'
'I was busy yaar!' he replied half-mindedly.
'Yeah I can see how busy you are,' replied Sudheer with a tone of sarcasm. Then Surya looked over Sudheer. His outfit was bedazzling.
'How much you bought this for?' Sudheer blushed and started twisting like a girl and said '500' with an awkward smile on his face. Surya was shocked. It was the same chocolate color leather jacket he had seen in the shop. Surya envied him. An elephant like Bharat seemed to be Lord Ganesha to him. He ran in search of Bharat. He didn't find him anywhere in the rooms. Finally, when he peeked from balcony, he found him getting away from the hostel. He ran with jet speed and caught him. Bharat with a wary and studying look asked, 'What happened Man! Why are you in such a hurry?'
'Dude! Tell me where did you buy that outfit for so less?' Bharat understood the situation. With a condescending tone using a bass voice, laying a hand over Surya's shoulder as if a father was taking a bloody lecture to his son when he was caught red-handedly smoking cigarettes, told 'You should have come with us instead of being all egoistic' and reverted to his way.

'Sorry dude! Never knew you are such talented. Just tell me the shop name'.

'Shop name is not enough. You need to have the talent of bargaining. You never had that', he laughed proudly. 'Well you can teach me'.

'Okay! On one condition! You have to arrange a meeting with that Russian girl' 'What! Russian girl?' Surya faked innocence.

'Come on Man! I saw Andria and you talking in the Bakery. You think no one observed? I was following you like Hutch dog till the beach. Bow!'

Surya was reminded of the dog with the old man which was barking all the way. It somehow sensed this disgusting creature eavesdropped on their conversation.

Surya gave a huge sigh, 'Just a meeting, right? Yeah, I will arrange', Bharat walked away proudly feeling his victory.

Surya while retreating to his room spotted Sudheer passing by. He was showing his new outfit to whoever he ran into. Surya held Sudheer and whispered something into his ears and put a hundred rupee note in his pocket.

Faizaan was searching for some address beside the old bus stand of Manali. The road was crowded. He turned on the Google Maps. He was up to something. There he found an old building with ghastly appearance which was looked after by an old man at the entrance with disheveled and weird appearance. He was looking pervertedly on each girl passing by. Faizaan went inside and brought something in his bag stealthily checking twice on either side if anyone was tracking him. Being confident that no one found him, he paced up and strode away.

Sudheer was tiptoeing behind him and grabbed Faizaan 'What was that?'

Faizaan was shocked on being caught and later he slowly moved close to him whispered, 'It's Mia Khalifa's porn CD She stopped acting in porn. Rare to find her exclusive videos'. Sudheer stared intently over the shop. His eyes dazzled thinking about something. He went close to the shop owner, grimly looking old man, and in the heights of excitement asked, 'Do you have Mallu Aunty video?', with a grin on his face unabashedly. The old man still looked for a moment which made Sudheer wonder if he was dead! Later he replied, 'We don't have the stalk; will let you know.'

'It's neither 'stalk' nor 'aakpaak karepaak' Sudheer jeered 'it's 'stock'.

'Why are you so worried about correcting him?' Faizaan apologized him. The old man asked sternly 'Give me your number'. Sudheer scribbled down his number and joined Faizaan.

Sudheer then called Surya secretly, 'Surya! Nothing to worry about. Faizaan was just about to show porn CD of Mia Khalifa. That's what he meant about surprise'.

Surya on the other side said, 'Thank God! I was worried what it would be otherwise' heaving a deep sigh of relief as if a bomb squad defused a bomb which was about to detonate.

Later that evening Surya and Bharat were sitting in the wooden cabin waiting for Andria. Surya promised the meeting and Bharat promised the bargaining. They were all set up for the master plan. Surya had not known much about the events that would set into motion. Bharat was so nervous. Every now and then he was asking Surya whether Andria would come. Surya by now learnt the art of ignoring him looking at the yonder. Bharat started biting his nails with nervousness. Surya felt all this a little over of him. He was expecting all these embarrassing episodes to end soon. 'I feel nervous man! What to do'.

'Macha! Take this vodka and have two shots'. Surya placed Vodka on the table.

'You are real friend yaar. You know what I need'. Bharat was about to kiss making his face a pout.

Surya just withheld Bharat from creating another embarrassing episode.

'Every time you say that, you realize that you were wrong'.

'Huh? What do you mean?'

'Nothing yaar. Enjoy the drink'.

Bharat had two shots quickly.

Soon Andria came in. She waved at Surya who was enchanted by her beauty. She was glittering with black colored skirt and white color top exposing her waist. Surya felt something falling on his hand. Bharat was gazing at her so intently, with his eyes wide open.

'Disgusting! Now I understand why you didn't get married even in your 30s. Shut your mouth Man! Stop gazing like that.' Surya warned in low tone. Andria joined them. 'What's up guys?'

Bharat took the initiative. 'You... hundred years! Just now...... Surya talking ...about your beauty', shouted Bharat breaking all syllables with series of pauses. Surya whispered into his ears.

'Dumbo! She is not deaf! Why are you shouting like that?'

'Sorry Man! Got nervous and confused about what to say! OMG! It's my first time to talk to a foreigner. It's so exciting'.

Surya looked at him as if he was a Zoo animal which lost from wild and joined the pack later without any surviving skills. 'How you still survive being so naive Man?' Surya pitied. Bharat ignored him. 'You know! Surya is a womanizer! Every time he walks, girls follow him'. Bharat looked at Surya expecting praise. Surya put a blank face wondering what he would say.

'Huh? Really? Tell me more', Andria asked curiously.

'Recently he went to Goa! You know what!' He was about to say something and became cautious. 'Anything happened in Goa stays in Goa! Ssshh!' He ended the sentence with a whistling sound.

'Yeah I heard about Goa!' Andria chuckled. 'It's famous for its spas and beaches'.

'Yeah, in a spa he got a variety massage.' Surya got bewildered with his last statement. He realized all this was a bad idea. He felt like he got stripped publicly just for an 'outfit'. Managing his mixed emotions of anger and embarrassment, he faked a smile at Andria.

'What massage?' laughed Andria looking at Surya for which he flabbergasted.

'Famous in Bangkok.' chuckled Bharat.

Surya whispered, 'Stop embarrassing yourself man. Tomorrow when you are reminded of all this, you will die of shame. You will regret this'.

Bharat ignored Surya and continued his monologue.

'Surya spent 20,000 rupees only'. 'Enough! Do I have to remember how you ended up with a transgender and spent sleepless nights the following weeks?' Surya hit the table hard and about to get up. Bharat became silent.

'Take it easy! Just for fun'. Andria soothed him by holding his hand. Surya controlled his anger and focused on her which relieved him from anxiety. She was bursting into laughter every time while Bharat made a funny comment. He got mesmerized with the beautiful smile of her. Recalled the time he spent with her in beach. He kept gazing at her while Bharat was releasing his precious monologue. Surya felt timeless.

The girl took out Charas and handed it to Surya 'You always wanted to try right? Try this'.

Surya hesitatingly took it. She lit it for him. Her face was glowing in that light. Her eyes looked so beautiful with a pink tinge on her cheeks. Surya took a deep puff and he felt the high. Everything seemed to be set in slow motion. On a slide glance, he looked at Bharat who was moving hands his up and down slowly with his jaws widely. Surya burst into laughter as he couldn't help it. It's Bharat's time to get puzzled.

The girl teased, 'You guys have no control over your feet, how can you slip off a girl's feet', winking at Surya.

Surya sobered up and looked steadily into her eyes holding her hands.

'Do you want me to show how?'

'Yeah! Show me', she provoked him.

Bharat fell on the table with a terrific thud.

Surya looked swiftly at Bharat and back on the girl saying 'okay'. Nothing seems to disturb them. They were deeply staring at each other slowly moving inch by inch toward each other by grabbing their right hands tighter every second. He put his left hand on her waist and held tightly.

She showed no resistance. In fact, she moaned a little that encouraged Surya. He slowly moved her away from the table and held her closely clamping his hands behind her waist. Surya landed his lips on hers. They started kissing. He tasted her body smell with his hands feeling her curves. She kept moaning and put her hands on his back. Later, gently she pushed him away.

'Looking eager to break civic laws?'

'Huh? I didn't understand'.

'Follow me'. She signaled him waving her index finger.

He followed her being spellbound.

She took him toward a room in a hostel. She went inside first and waved him to come inside.

He lifted her weight and passionately kissed her. Later they were on the floor. Surya exclaimed! 'OMG! I don't have condoms.'

'Don't worry. I have in my purse'.

Surya widened his eyes. The girl chuckled, rolling her eyes toward her purse. Surya tore one and made out with her. Grasping for breathing while making out, Surya told, 'I love you!'

'Do you talk this pillow talk to every girl?'

'No. I really mean it. I feel pleasant and timeless in your company as if I am spellbound'

Slowly, both of them moved rhythmically when Surya came inside her and fell aside on bed. Both were laughing at each other. Surya remarked 'It is the best day in Manali'.

'Maybe it's the best day of your life.' She eyed on him teasingly. Slowly they dozed off.

There was a moment of silence.

Later when he checked her. She was asleep. She looked so beautiful. He gently moved her hair aside and kissed her cheeks. He spooned her and slept all night being stuck to her.

CHAPTER SEVEN

THE CANCER GIRL

The next day when he woke, she was not on his side. Surya assumed she might have gone. He checked his phone leisurely for any notifications. Yawned. Got out from his bed and bent over the balcony. He could see Bharat still sleeping on the table. Surya recalled the incidents happened the day before. He swore Bharat for all the embarrassment he created. Every morning he had a habit of jogging. Now his body craves for some workout. He went on to the streets of Old Manali and jogged against the steep. It was a good workout. He passed over the leather outfit shop. He was reminded of the deal he made with Bharat. However, with the interesting twist of the event with the Russian girl, he just gave upon the idea to hang out with Bharat! He recalled the body scent of Andria. The mere thought of her passed chills in his body. He felt so blessed to have fucked her the night before. 'How to contact her? What if she was Kashmiri terrorist and seducing me to become a Human bomb? Or an assassin sent by my seniors to kill me?' He convinced himself not to overthink. Observing small kids passing on the footpath of the road made his control over his thoughts much easier. Their pleasant smile made him feel good. He returned to the hostel being tired and drenched with sweat. He did some pushups and routine workouts in balcony near his room.

Chakradhar spotted him. 'Good morning Surya! Good day! You are making me feel jealous with your determination to workout'.

'Thank you'. Surya said absentmindedly preoccupied with his pushups.

Bharat came out from his room. It's 9 AM. He pointed at his watch indicating it's getting late. Surya nodded and went inside to freshen up. They were planning for River Rafting. Someone shouted 'courier'. It's a courier guy who came to deliver a package to Surya. He was surprised.

Who would send him a courier? Only a few knew his location. He went down to receive the delivery and looked inside. It's a CD. Luckily the hotel provides a TV and a DVD player with each room. So, he went inside and played it being surprised what it was. The TV didn't turn on. What could be the CD about? He was curious about it. Neha was passing by to check what's going on. Surya was shaking the TV vigorously in a desperate attempt to turn it on. 'Hello! Why are you so bothered about the TV now?', Neha asked, while drying her hair with a towel. Surya acknowledged her presence. She was wearing a t-shirt and jeans.

'Yeah it's nothing! I just got a parcel with CD in it. I am checking what it is', replied Surya. 'Maybe you will have to wait for the power to come back. Otherwise why do you think I took shower with cold water?' She shrugged.

'Oh shit! Then I have to wait for the Power' Surya told out of exasperation.

Bharat interfered. 'Come on Surya! It's getting late. Get ready! Fast! We have to take the Bus'.

Surya gave rest to the matters on the table and started to get ready for the trip. They had planned the itinerary well. The plan was to go to the nearby Beas River for River Rafting. His phone beeped.

It's a message from Andria that she would come to his room. He riveted his eyes thinking about what to do. He feigned some discomfort in his stomach by holding hands over his tummy and asked them to carry on with the plan and excuse him.

'Is everything okay? Surya!' Bharat asked.

'Yeah! May be a little sick. It's okay. You guys carry on. I have no mood for River rafting' Surya told feigning discomfort in his face.

'It's okay then, we see you later. Take care' Bharat said being concerned.

Neha, Kiran, Bharat and Chakradhar went away.

Surya went to take a nap when he heard the banging on the door. Surya shouted 'Who is it?'

'Mr. Surya! We are from CBI. I have come to know you have stolen something so precious. We have come here to arrest you' a harsh lady voice ended with a grumble.

'Surya wake up!'

Surya was so frightened. 'What! Mam, what are you talking about? I don't understand what you are saying'.

'Come on Surya! Don't try to act smart! We have information that you are stealing things from innocent girls. If you don't open it, we have to break it open!'

'Innocent girls? When I was in the 2nd standard, I stole a pencil from my classmate but she was not innocent', Surya winked.

'Stop the Bullshit and open the door, or else I have to break it'.

'Then break it ... or do I have to smuggle any hammer for that?' Surya chuckled at his lame joke.

The girl lowered her voice accepting her defeat, beseeched him in a pleading familiar tone 'Come on Surya! Just open it! I forgot something important'. Surya puzzled and looked around in the room. There was a linger underwear over the bed. He chuckled.

'Requesting? That's good. It's improvement'. He opened the door. Andria was standing there waving her hand with a pretended anger. She just pushed him away and took a seat on his bed. 'Why did you come? For me or for that?' He showed her underwear and chuckled. She pounced over him playfully punching over his chest, she nudged his shoulder pretending an argument. 'You stole an innocent girl's heart and now acting so innocent?' 'Innocent? You keep condoms in your purse and saying innocent?' He bantered on her while she made her eyes into bulb and punched him whimsically.

He came closely and clamped his hands around her. She looked steadily into his face. 'Something is cooking up in your head'.

He was about to kiss her when she turned her head aside closing his lips. 'Does your battery ever die?' She slowly let lose herself from his grip. 'Just get ready, we need to go out! I have to show you something', she said and gently pushed him into the washroom. He was saying something but she didn't listen. After some time, he came out after having a shower. She was waiting impatiently and was glad to see Surya finish his shower. 'Great! Let's go'. She grabbed his hands and took him out. 'Wait! Andria', Surya yelled.... Neha who was passing by looked at him and chuckled. Andria was surprised why she was laughing. She gave a glimpse over him and closed her mouth with her hands out of shock. He was on his underwear! Out of sheer embarrassment he shut the doors over her face. She looked helplessly being flabbergasted at Neha! Neha shrugged her shoulder and went inside. In a moment Surya came out closing the zip of his Jerkin with a pretended anger. She rose her eyebrows.

'What's the matter?' Surya asked.

'Shut up!'

'What?'

'Your pant Zip...'.

He embarrassedly turned other side and closed his zip. She guided him to some place. It was written 'Sarojini Hospital' over the hospital. 'Now what? Why have you brought me here?' Surya asked her impatiently wearing off his helmet.

'Urgently! You need to donate blood' and grabbed him hurriedly pulling into the hospital

'What? Why do I have to?' He set free from her hands with an annoyed look.

'I will give you explanations later.' She said impatiently and grasped his hands and dragged him inside.

'But Andria! I never gave blood! I am frightened with needles' saying this, he almost cried like a kid pulling himself out of her grip. She gyrated toward him and asked whimsically 'Are you really a doctor? What are you saying?'

'Well, I was an expert in pricking needles but not in getting pricked', said hesitantly hiding his face.

Andria dragged him up to the blood bank. She put a stern look on her face and asked blatantly folding her hands, 'Will you do it or not?'

'No!' He turned away his face, folding his hands as if a child prevented his mother to feed.

'I know you would say something... like that', he became suspicious. She removed a knife from her purse and pointed toward Surya. 'You told you were frightened about needles, right? Let's see what you are more frightened about.'.

'Andria! Come on! No time for jokes' Surya chuckled whimsically.

'Proceed Surya! Or else I will stab you'. Surya just relaxed, stood steadily and looked into her eyes and stepped closer to her. She was stunned with sudden events. He slowly came near to her and took the knife from her, kissed on her cheek. She left her mouth ajar with eyes made into bulb. The hospital staff and blood donors were looking at them fascinatedly, especially one donor who stopped pressing his smiley ball out of curiosity.

'You don't need to stab! You have already stabbed in my heart' and he took an inclined seat. Andria riveted her eyes aside with a cunning smile. The technician poked his needle into his skin, but Surya stayed motionless gazing deeply into her eyes. The technician was observing them and later joined his colleagues who were giggling.

Surya came out of the room, asked intently, 'Why do you want blood for?' She took her to a room silently and showed a patient. There was a man, pale and lean with sunken eyes lying on his bed, with a mass on his left cheek.

'Okay! Is that Mukesh? And you are about to take lecture on Smoking? If it's the case, tell me I will run from here', Surya said closing his ears turning away. She knocked into his stomach with her elbow,

'See the child' a 10-year-old female kid, with a pale face, shaved head, sunken eyes with an oxygen mask, was laid on the beside bed. Her mother sat beside her while caressing her. Andria knocked the door. The child cast her eyes over her instantaneously and flickered a smile on her withered face. A yellow colored fluid was connected to her through IV lines. Andria took him beside the kid. She stooped over her on her right side and caressed on her head gently and stood erect to face Surya and told, 'See Surya! You have been bled to donate blood for this kid. Her name is Mary. She is having leukemia and was on her Chemotherapy!'

Surya observed the Child. She was having three tattoos of love symbol on her right forearm. He looked pitifully over her. 'What were they?' Surya asked showing her tattoos. She looked at her tattoos.

'They were her victory tattoos' and looked into his eyes 'Mary went on chemo thrice and successfully cured. So, she got 3 tattoos'. Surya looked contemplatively.

'Never think low about your profession. If you can be a good surgeon, you can treat people like Mary and help them. You got a gift, use it. There is a lot of professional satisfaction in it. I want you to know how beautiful it is to selflessly help others and add value to their life. This world is a beautiful place Surya and we were so gifted to live here. Stop complaining and appreciate the beauty of it'. Surya looked at her innocent face which was smiling without any worry about the next day. 'See, for her life is a gift. And she wants to live the last days happily' and she turned to Surya. 'For you it had been a burden. Just develop the perspective of her. See with Mary's eyes. Live your life to the fullest every moment'. Surya felt his epiphany touched again. Andria was so caring about him and he didn't find such a person before. He smiled gently and nodded in approval.

CHAPTER EIGHT

THE SOCIAL NIGHT

In the evening, Surya was waiting for Andria near the Hostel gate. It was around 8 PM. She came after an hour. She was wearing a single piece sleeveless bedazzling black dress, extending up to an inch above the knee.

'Why are you so late?'

'Sorry! I got busy with some work. Anyhow the dance starts around 9 PM'.

'You should have told, right?' Surya asked angrily.

'I thought you knew. Even I was going for the first time to the place'. She shrugged.

They headed towards Over the Moon Restaurant. She went ahead, while he was parking the bike him that she would meet in the restaurant. He parked his bike in parking slot while she took the lift in cellar. She was shocked which floor she had to go as it was her first time in that restaurant and clicked on the lift buttons. Nothing worked. The lights turned off. She started sweating a lot, with her heart rate increasing with slight chest pain, her hands began to tremor. She had this problem since childhood. These episodes occur occasionally. Exact trigger of the attack was either enclosed or dark places. She almost collapsed on the floor. She groped for a Propranolol tablet that she kept in her purse, which would be helpful in such a moment. She took it for her relief and the episode subsided. Again, the lights turned on and the lift took her automatically to the 8th floor. When she entered into the restaurant, it was fully occupied by so many people. At the center, there was bar counter, around a huge round wide pillar on which the Menu of the available beverages was written. She was already sweaty with that Black sleeveless dress and looked grotesque in that whole place. She looked for Surya. As he was not there, she shifted to a table nearby a social dance performance. A young guy in his formals and with charming look invited her for a dance. She accepted his invitation and involved in the dance. In the meantime, Surya came to that place, he couldn't find her so he shifted his focus onto the Beers. But it was so difficult to read the Menu over the wide round pillar as half of the letters were on the other side of the pillar. Surya helplessly revolved around the pillar to read the menu. He looked like a lost kid in a procession. His favorite was Apple Cider. He asked the Bartender 'One Apple Cider please'. 'Sorry Sir, it's not available this time'.

Now Surya was confused about what he had to take. He saw two guys drinking freshly brewed beer over the counter. It's creamy color looked like pineapple juice except the plenty of froth over the surface which confirmed it was beer. Another Bartender was serving that beer to those guys. Surya tempted to drink that. He asked, 'What was it? Draught Beer?' 'Yes sir! Do you want?'

'Yeah, please give me one', he said and hoped that beer would calm him a bit.

'Small, Medium or Large?'

Surya didn't hear properly but felt weird to ask again.

'Give me anything'. Surya told so naively as he was confused.

Bartender gave a pitiful look as if Surya had been first time for any Pub. He took a tiny glass and was about to pour the freshly brewed Beer coming right away from the pipeline controlled by a tap. Surya wondered why was he giving so less quantity and argued with the Bartender

'No no! What are you giving in that?' He annoyingly pointed out to mini glass which might have a capacity of 50 ml.

'Relax Sir! Just taste it'. He held the mini glass toward Surya.

'Hmm... good. Give me medium' Bartender pointed big jug as he couldn't hear properly what Surya said in the midst of loud noise.

Surya anxiously said, 'No no... that one' he pointed to 500 ml mug wondering what he would do with a jug of Pitcher.

When he was tasting the Beer, Andria came. 'What are you doing here? Come on!'

Surya was embarrassed to answer as he completely forgot about her and followed her to the social dance.

Surya somehow settled with her at a table. But he was so nervous with the series of events happened. Spanish songs were playing on the background. So many couples were stepping to their moves in sync with the music. Andria was dancing with random guys on their invitation. One of the guys was so intriguing for Surya. He was a tall fair guy with some sort of innocence in his face, with a disproportionate body as if all the fat in his body was shifted to his waist. Good thing about that guy was that he wouldn't allow his imperfect appearance affect his confidence. It's what you call beauty inside. Surya was reminded of the movie 'The Beautiful Mind' in which the hero was a schizophrenic but still had a good heart.

Surya was lost in his thoughts. His experience with this adventure club, the memories made with his new friends, the dance, the trek, the night hangouts, the passion of exploring new places meeting new people felt so surreal. It's a kind of escape from his family. These people who he was travelling are not judgmental. They accepted the way he was. They have no expectations and are least bothered about reforming him. He recalled Neha, Bharat, Chakradhar, and Sudheer. It was a pleasant time chilling with beer and girls. It's so different from his stressful life in Hyderabad. His family was so judgmental with an ultimate goal to reform him. Surya himself felt so perfect but the way people judged him with trivial incidents and controversies dismayed him.

Recently, he was involved in the trap of a girl, his subordinate. She initiated the conversation, asked for his Instagram. Surya started texting with her. She asked about the girls he was hanging out. She had rivalry with one girl who he hung out with. She told negatively about the girl that she stole her phone. She asked why he hadn't got married instead of hanging out with girls. He felt offensive. What right did she have to poke on his personal life? Being frustrated, he texted that 'Marriage takes time. I am having an active social life so that I don't get desperate with girls. If I get desperate ultimately you will suffer'. And that girl took a screenshot of that and showed it to the HOD. He called her parents and told badly against him.

His life changed ever since. His parents were constantly nagging about the incident and started policing him. He was grounded at his home and wasn't allowed to hang out with his friends on weekends as his friends are outside his profession. What was the logic in not meeting with his non-medico friends and especially girls? If he was more restrained, he would be more frustrated and text girls in social media to compensate for emptiness. Ultimately texting girls would lead to every problem similar to what he was having then.

There was so much tension with his family. One day he was having a driving test. His day began badly. When he drove his car out of his home in reverse gear, he hadn't opened the gate completely. So, he got stuck in the middle. He absentmindedly drove the car out. The front bumper was damaged by crashing with the gate while he was gyrating the wheels. It felt like a bad omen. He had that thought constantly nagging in his mind. He was so worried what his parents would say. He didn't know how to cope up with such mental torture. Somehow, he convinced himself that he would get his car repaired after the driving test and things would be the way it was before. It would cost him but it's a lot better than constant nagging of his mother. When he reached the RTA office, he got a call from his mother arguing about the incident. Surya thought his mother hadn't seen and all those incidents would go unnoticed. But once he got the call from his mother, he had felt so much guilt and shame. He had to give a driving test too at the moment. When he was about to give his test, he got a message from his brother to delete a WhatsApp status. It was regarding the day before Salsa event he had been with his friends. He put a hashtag 'Love Salsa'. His brother wanted to remove it as it would show people that he had been enjoying with girls and wouldn't get married. That irritated him so badly. He went into a rivalry with him the moment through texting. It affected his level of attention and concentration. He wondered how he would perform his driving test. He was waiting in the line for his turn. He observed previously how to do it by watching others doing it. His turn came eventually. He steadily and slowly, in the first gear finished the patterns of 8 and H. He passed the test fortunately. When he came home, he had been involved in a hot argument with his brother and had never talked with him since then.

Surya knew few basics of Salsa but that he would never be sufficient to give a performance confidently with a girl. And Salsa gave somewhat bad memories with his family though he loved the art. So, he kept watching other guys doing Salsa especially Andria and her random partners. At one moment he saw those guys touching her waist holding her closer. Surya teleported himself to being with her, dancing together instead of that guy. He felt so jealous that he wanted to stop the guy but it would have created a scene. So, he refrained his urge of smashing the fellow.

Soon, a lady sat opposite to him on a chair. She looked so tired after dancing a lot. But still she was getting invitations to dance and she continued dancing with jest. Surya was sitting alone while she initiated the conversation.

'What is so motivating to you? The dance or the girls?' She winked. Surya became alert. His own thoughts were drowning him. That soft but confident voice was so relieving for him. He looked at her face. She looked beautiful with sleeveless shirt exposing her waist and torn jeans. She was tall and attractive. Surya winked, 'Yeah! Obviously, girls'.

'You know what? You truly enjoy when you do the dance instead of watching these girls'.

'Never agree with anything else more. I was kidding before actually'.

'Come on. Let's do!' She passed her hand as an invitation for dance with a gentle smile and told whimsically 'you don't learn by sitting and watching.'

Surya was thrilled to dance with her. It's the first time he had ever done Salsa with a partner. Kind of nervous but still excited. She held her hands in semi-flexed and prone position and placed her palms over his hands which was in semi-flexed but supine position. Surya began dancing to her cues.

'Front' the lady was tutoring. Surya was dancing one step forward and one step back complementary to her moves.

'Side! Left... in place! Right... in place'.

'Back! Left... in place! Right... in place'.

Shift your weight along with move'.

Surya was enjoying dance with her. She was smiling gently with proper eye contact. So surreal and impressed with the lady's confidence. 'You are doing pretty well as a beginner. Just keep practicing'. These words boosted the spirit of Surya.

He later sat on the chair being tired, facing the woman. She asked out of curiosity 'What do you do?'

'I am a General Surgeon. What about you?'

'Oohhoo! General Surgeon! Even my father was General Surgeon. I am a lawyer for last 28 years'.

Surya shocked, drank a glass of water and responded a moment later relieving from the effect it made on him 'So you might have started your practice since you are 2 years old' winked Surya.

The lady laughed and told, 'Not 2 but 22'.

Surya was calculating her age on an imaginary abacus as if he was solving some IIT problem. 'So, your age is 50 years!' Surya exclaimed. She looked like she was in her 30s.

'How do you know Andria?' she asked inquisitively

'I just met her few days back' still absorbed in the shock.

He looked at Andria dancing on the dance floor. She was like a dish of butter garlic lobster everyone craved, but only few could afford.

'You don't even know her much and you have been hanging out with her. You know what?', she came closer and whispered into his ears. 'You are an easy target for terrorists' mocked him with laughter.

'Yeah I know. I felt a sort of thrill having sex with a terrorist. My mind is ticking like a time bomb every time I see her. She might have inserted a time bomb indeed', he winked.

'By the way I am Raavi D'cruz', she shook her hands with him. 'You did it! You are so fast. You don't look so'.

'Hello Madam! Don't judge a book by its cover'.

'I am intrigued to ask you one thing'.

'Yeah. Shoot!'

'Is that love or lust?'

'I am not sure. I feel timeless with her company.'. Surya laughed and had a glance on Andria. She was so involved in dancing with some guy. It felt so beautiful to look at her smile but sensed some trouble behind it. Surya had the feeling that whoever he would get closer would leave him eventually. So, he developed this attitude of living in the moment, love unconditionally and expect nothing. As he was gazing at her she threw a glance at him. By then she finished her dance with her partner and gave a 'high five'. She gestured to him to come up for dance. Surya hesitated initially but wanted to give a try. 'You can't learn by just sitting and watching'. He mustered all his courage and paired up with her. She took his left hand and gently let it land on her waist while other hand on her palm. He slowly got involved with the moment. He was dancing rhythmically to music with her, following her cues, spinning her with the rhythm of music. He forgot everything else. It didn't matter even if the world ends up at that moment.

Surya felt like spending some more time with her. While they were leaving, Surya had seen Raavi who involved in a dance with a guy. He looked over his shoulder and bid bye. She gave a gentle smile being involved in her dance.

'I hope you didn't get bored. I don't know you are such a good dancer', Andria told apologetically.

'Thank you. I was not bored. The old woman gave good company'.

'Which old woman? Raavi? She is so beautiful, right?'

Surya still struck by her presence, her charm and her looks. 'Yeah, she is 50!' Surya exclaimed.

'OMG! 50! I can't believe it'.

'I felt jealous with those guys who danced with you' She winked. She laughed and playfully hit her head on shoulders and placed it there. She looked haughtily and smiled pleasantly.
Chatting with her was increasingly relaxing and devoid of anxiety. He could survive being a general surgeon and having her as his girlfriend. He was staring somewhere contemplating deeply. 'What?' She broke into his thoughts. 'Nothing. I am imagining how you would be looking at your 50. More precisely how many teeth do you have?' Surya bared his teeth widely like Hyena!
Andria opened her mouth wide in exclamation, made her eyes widened and slapped his wrist with pretended anger.
Raavi was watching them until Surya disappeared followed by Andria

CHAPTER NINE

THE DREAM

That was an old house in a village, barely built of bricks. A small family was living in that house in two small rooms in a kutcha house– one kitchen and one hall room with 3 kids. It was raining outside with dark clouds covering the sky with no chance of visibility of the sun. The kids were running in that home outside in the rain. One kid, the elder one of 10 years age, went out to water plants which were present a few feet outside the front door. It was raining but still doing that. He came back into the room scurrying all through the way with inevitable drenching in the rain. The kid was doing nothing more. Just watering plants in spite of the rain, scurrying back home being wet, repeatedly as an obsession to pass time not knowing anything else to do. The room inside was gloomy with power cut and none inside. So void and alone. His heartbeat was increasing with his every scream reverberating inside the rooms, hoping someone would come to his rescue, being scared to death. He hastened his activity of watering to curb his fear with not much help. Suddenly, he fell down, crying aloud but no one was hearing in that dark gloomy day.

Surya woke up from his dream. Sat cross-legged over his bed, riveted to one side to hangover both his legs from the edge of the bed with both his hands grasping the edge tightly, gasping for breath. He was sleeping alone. Andria left for her place the before day. He felt so lonely and his nightmare reflected his state of mind.

The next day on arrival of dawn early in the morning, not that early but 8 AM which was considered early for youth, especially on holidays. Surya planted a knock-on Bharat's door. Bharat didn't open the door. Surya persisted. 'The lust on the Russian obviously made you blind Surya Aryan Seth', Bharat's voice boomed from the corridor. Surya took a double take on Bharat and single one back on the door he was pounding his fists. The door was latched from outside. Bharat gave a grin baring his teeth like hyena twisting his finger one side of his head like loosening a fictitious screw. 'You know what Surya, I am in hurry to meet my Tinder date, but then again brother code says, you supersede all', Surya smiled and moved aside while Bharat unlatched the door. Bharat went toward his cupboard shuffling his t-shirts looking for particular one. Bharat took out a red colored t-shirt. 'I feel like I am in love', said Surya hesitatingly whether to disclose the information doubting his pillars of trust on Bharat.

'Dove? Sorry, I don't have one', Bharat said absentmindedly scrounging through his clothes.

Surya was preparing to leave thinking that was a bad idea.

'What, say again, you are in Love? UN-BE-LEAVE-ABLE!' Bharat faced Surya in astonishment, holding a pair of socks. 'But I am so confused dude. What if she is not in love with me? What if...', Surya clearly flustered with his voice faltering.

Bharat looked sympathetically. 'See man! Sometimes you have to follow your heart. There is nothing wiser than that. Risk is everywhere, accept the risk!' riveting toward the door. 'I am in a hurry. Don't take wrong'. Bharat's face contorted reflecting difficulty in handling the situation. 'Have to catch up with my date, Man. She might be waiting for me at CCD. See you soon. Good luck'. 'Thanks for your suggestion Bharat', Surya looked unto him with gratitude. He took charge of his emotions and followed him to the door. 'Good luck to you too, Man'.

'Luck is my desperate wife Man. It never leaves me', Bharat winked at Surya who laughed with regained enthusiasm.

CHAPTER TEN

THE MYSTERIOUS CD

Surya was waiting for Andria outside her residence Hotel Elite. He was looking desperately toward his watch while sitting on his bike surrounded by early morning fog.

He got a call from Sudheer, 'Bhai! Are you bringing the CD? 'Yeah I am bringing the CD.'

Sudheer implored Surya the night before to bring a CD from the old Manali shop which was the same shop Faizaan once visited; it looked dark and gloomy. A fat lady was sitting behind a rack on which CDs of different films were laid. Surya flustered. 'Sudheer, I am going to kill you!' Surya thought in his head. He was so tensed and fidgeting before he could utter a simple word 'Mallu'. She looked so ferocious as if he had asked her to elope with him. She bent down in her place. Surya looked aghast wondering if she would take out a broomstick and beat him. He was prepared to run. She brought out a CD and placed it on the counter. '50 rupees', she said in a stern voice. He took the CD, placed 100 Rupees and went away avoiding any eye contact with her, not even waiting for the change. The next day, he reached Andria's guest house.

There was no sign of Andria coming out of her room. He tried to call her, but she was not picking up the call. Surya didn't fathom what to do. So, he opened the gate slowly and went inside. The lawn in entrance contained a swing suspended from a rod connecting two triangular rods.

Passing the narrow path in the lush green lawn, he opened a door to the guest house. He wondered how she could afford such a costly

Duplex house with her mere income. In the living, two creamy colored sofas with rhombus-shaped pillows welcomed him with two giant windows shadowing them.

The mellow shaped early morning Sun rose from its horizon with its rays striking Surya. The window curtains, partially covering the window, dazzled red with the glow. His heart rose with delight with the appreciation of the ambiance.

He rested on the sofa, laid his arm over the back of the Sofa, with a surreal feeling. He could hear someone showering inside. She was humming songs. He lingered through the room, observing the well decorated shelves. Something shiny held his attention. His eyes widened with the careful inspection. It was exactly the same CD that he got as courier.

Why Andria tried to hide it. Who sent it? Why did he/she send it to me? What is its content? These questions popped up in his head. Suddenly, he heard the creak of the washroom door. He hid the CD in his bag and replaced it with the CD he brought.

Wrapped in a towel, drying her hair and humming a melody, Andria came out of her washroom. Her mouth fell opened with shock. She tottered meekly toward him with hesitancy.

She flustered with some anxiety. Andria was hiding something from him, from the way she looked.

'Just wait for me outside', she nudged him out of her room, latched it behind him and checked the CD. She puffed a deep sigh of relief. Her towel heaved over her bosom like water waves on a sea. She freshened up. She wore a maroon sleeveless single piece extending one inch about the knee and matching Latin shoes.

She opened the door with a smile, pounced upon him, put her hands around his neck and kissed him apologizing 'Sorry baby, for making you wait!' Surya smiled back and both of them went away on his bike to the waterfalls he planned that day.

CHAPTER ELEVEN

THE PINK MAN

A bunch of UNO cards were distributed among the team members. Faizaan and Sudheer sat along with Kiran and Neha under a shed beside a house. They went on a trek to Hampta pass, but the gates were closed. Out of disappointment, they headed back down the hills doing a mini trek while Surya was enjoying his time in Manali exploring the nearby places. At lunch time, they stopped by a small dhaba. It was a beautiful place with a house with few rooms on one side attached to the road and open plain area with grass on the other side. They were all so hungry. Sudheer and Faizaan ordered Bread–Omelet while the girls ordered Maggi. Neha had a plan of playing UNO. She distributed cards to everyone seven each. The first player has to put his card in between. The next person has to throw a card either of same color or same number. If he didn't have a card to place, he has to pick one card from the rest of the bundle of cards spared after distributing, which was kept beside the scattered cards. There were few powers in the cards. Had a person thrown a power card, the next person would have to comply with what had been written on it. Suppose if the power card had been 2+, the next person would have to pick up 2 cards. If it had been 'skip', next player would have no chance in that round, for 'color change', next player would have to put the card of mentioned color. Eventually who threw away all the cards would be the winner and shouldn't forget mentioning UNO on last card before someone caught otherwise you should pick up seven cards again. Faizaan had a 'color change' card which he used and ordered the shift to 'pink'.

All of them burst into laughter. There was no pink color, only blue, green, yellow and red were available.

Neha who sat against Faizaan mocked him, 'Dude! Where was pink? It was red man'.

'I think he got color blindness'; Kiran added to the mockery while sitting to the left of Neha. Both of them gave a girly giggle, of course Kiran looked more like feigning it hardly. Sudheer patted his hand over Faizaan's thigh laughing with a grin on his face, sitting left to Faizaan. Chakradhar was sitting some other side lonely being absorbed into thoughts with a Cigarette in his mouth, occasionally glancing at them, ignoring as that was all a childish game.

Faizaan invited Chakradhar, 'Come on Bhai! You can also join. There is a room for you too'.

'No thanks Man! I am enjoying my Cigarette and solitude. You guys carry on'.

They were all waiting for a vehicle which has to come and pick them to Manali 50 km away from the place. It was 4 PM and the Sun was almost hidden behind clouds as he was playing hide and seek with earth. There were tall trees on the other side of the road opposite to the old house with the trunks swaying and the leaves rustling to the orchestra played by the wind.

Faizaan picked again a 'color shift' power card and used it saying 'color change to pink'. Neha teased 'Why are you so obsessed with pink Man'.

'I think Pink is his favorite color', added Kiran giving a high-five to Neha.

Sudheer chuckled with his hands covering his mouth for which Faizaan gave a grim look and Sudheer stopped laughing.

'I was just confused with red and pink as pink was too obvious everywhere'

'Where do you see so much pink?' giggled Neha.

Faizaan paused for a second contemplating what to say, he explained, 'See, your shoes are pink, your kerchief was pink and... your lipstick was also pink'.

'I didn't put any lipstick today'.

'Yeah, you might not put lipstick, but still your lips were pink right?', winked Faizaan. 'So, you are ogling at her while we are playing' Kiran teased. Neha felt sudden flush of pink on her cheeks. She ordered Kiran, 'Come on... start playing!' trying to divert the topic.

A small lamb came into the scene. Neha, with an air of excitement stood up and went after the lamb being fascinated by it. Faizaan followed her. Kiran and Sudheer exchanged looks. Neha was holding the lamb and giving girly poses. Faizaan took out his camera and was taking snaps of her. She was changing her pose, one time cuddling the lamb, other time kissing it, every instant waiting for Faizaan to capture her pictures. The lamb was fond of nibbling the fingers with its toothless mouth, even Neha was enjoying it by putting her finger inside the lamb's mouth. Faizaan was enjoying taking pictures of her. She looked so adorable to him. He was complimenting her beauty every time he got a chance. Neha reflected with a cute smile thanking him. Faizaan gestured Sudheer to come, Sudheer dropped his pack of cards and joined Faizaan. He gave his camera to Sudheer and pleaded with him to take their pictures. Sudheer raised his eyebrow with protest. Faizaan pleaded with him holding his chin. Sudheer accepted with a condition that he had to give a treat in bar that night after reaching Manali. Faizaan accepted to the terms and joined Neha as her partner in photography. He took it as a great chance to get closer to her, touching her finger as a pretext to hold the lamb. When Neha was holding the lamb high, he gestured to handle it to him. While taking the lamb he brushed her bosom which was prominent behind her tight black t-shirt, with his elbow. Neha felt that but didn't protest as if nothing happened. He tilted his head closer to Neha, when he happened to see her cleavage from an angle. Faizaan felt shy to peek at them but couldn't refrain from staring occasionally. Sudheer was observing everything, winking at Faizaan whenever he caught him looking at her cleavage. He felt a surge of hormones flowing in his blood. Neha was playfully throwing the lamb in the air and catching it, as if she was playing catch–catch with a pleasant smile on her

face, 'It's so cute right?' and turned her face toward him.
'Yeah really!' She caught him looking upon to her cleavage, 'Hello!' Faizaan instantly fluttered his eyes away. 'Look at the lamb! Not somewhere else' and mocked him playfully. Faizaan blushed, smiled awkwardly, and scratched his head helplessly, with a grin on his face. Neha was enjoying the way his face contorted into different expressions and smiled with her eyes staring down trying to hide her feelings, moving her hair aside. Faizaan moved aside, gestured his hand towards a way into the landscape suggesting for a quiet walk. Neha nodded with a smile and a blush on her cheeks, casting her eyes down. They went on a walk.
'It's so beautiful climate, right?' Faizaan mumbled being troubled how to start a small talk.
'Yeah. It's so good'
'I wanted to ask you for a long time. What's your opinion about me?'
'We met only for a week. How would that be a long time?' Faizaan laughed nervously. Neha continued. 'You are a good guy, care about your friends, Good leader, seeing you the way you help others while doing treks'.
'Yeah! Thank you. I don't know that', couldn't help hiding the blush on his face.
'Your wife will be so lucky', Neha teased playfully.
'Why don't you be that lucky girl then?' Faizaan replied ignoring the sarcasm.
'Huh?' Neha raised her eyebrows bulging her eyes'.
'Seriously, I have feelings for you. Just don't know how to share'.
Neha stood silent. Faizaan came close to her, occupying her personal space. Gently raised her chin and looked into her eyes. She didn't resist. That look had passed goose pimples down his body. He kissed her lips gently.
Faizaan approached closer to Sudheer making a pout motioning his lips as in a kiss. Sudheer was stunned by the sudden change of events for which he instantly pushed him away violently to avoid the most embarrassing incident. Faizaan came out of the day dreaming with a stunned expression. All those guys were enjoying

watching him, chuckling silently at the way his facial expressions molded on his face. Faizaan looked aghast. Suddenly, everyone chortled into laughter. 'Thank heavens, he didn't kiss Sudheer. Sudheer you have to throw a party for consummating your relationship', Neha broke into laughter falling aside on Kiran.

'Hey pink man! Who was with you in your dreams? Pink woman or another pink man or Sudheer?' Again, Neha burst into laughter. Faizaan grinned abashedly.

One thing Neha observed so fascinatedly was that place doesn't have a refrigerator.

If any of the customers ordered for cool drinks, of course most would prefer tea or coffee; but if in case someone ordered Cool drinks, an 18-year-old kid would come bringing those lukewarm drinks, get relieved from his encumbrance under cold running water which was flowing into landscape. He kept it there for some time so that the drinks would cool down. Neha called that 18-year-old kid having thin lean athletic body, high cheek bones and good height, and invited him to sit beside her. He turned out to be funny and those guys were enjoying his company knowing more about the place, their lifestyle. On the other side, a tinge of jealous took charge on Faizaan, but he still acted playfully, deploying his strategies to keep the kid busy, by ordering food to keeping him off her premises which put a big hole in his pocket and pressure on his belly buttons. Neha was observing him suspiciously. The family was so good with their hospitality. They all reflected them with good wishes, had some pictures with Neha posing with the two-family dogs and the lamb. That's when they heard the sound of the vehicle which they hired to pick up, arrived there. Everyone with an enhanced sense of elation, embarked the vehicle. Neha sat beside Faizaan whispered cheerfully, 'What's that?' Faizaan perplexed.

'You are acting a little weird today'.

Faizaan faltered, 'Nothing. Everything's good'.

'Fine', Neha looked away.

'You were the one in my dream'

Neha blushed. She acted as if she didn't hear. Faizaan flabbergasted and looked away.

CHAPTER TWELVE

THE HIDDEN TRUTH

Surya came back to the room from waterfalls at 10 AM. Exhausted. His eyes fell on the CD in his bag. He reached the far end of the room beside the bed, played the CD in the DVD player in his room and relaxed himself in the Sofa facing the TV.

Some glittering visuals appeared on the screen. The video commenced showing a duplex bungalow with lush green lawn with full of shrubs and trees. The sky appeared dark with the sounds of beetles resonated in the wind the area. Along the paved way of cobbled stones from the gate to the entrance of the mansion, a BMW car pulled over to its parking slot in the basement. A young man, 6 feet tall, blond Caucasian, with robust physique and handsome with clean shaven face, in his blue colored formal dress with maroon tie and shoes stepped down from the car. Being exhausted, pulled his tie free with frustration he walked inside his house.

Surya connected with the character as it resembled to his professional life. He took his seat opposite in his sofa. It felt like a Hollywood movie.

The man passed inside the hall room, took the stairs at the middle of the duplex building. He called his wife while taking stairs.

'Dear! Where are you? I am waiting for you'

Sorry honey, I am busy in work. I will come late today. He looked at the clock. It struck 10 PM. He slowly unlatched his bedroom door and fell on his bed. He heard the footstep sounds from the corridor. The footsteps disappeared increased in its intensity and disappeared in a minute.

There was eerie note to the scene. Surya immediately dialed Sudheer. Sudheer, who was busy in buying another jerkin, bargaining for a reasonable price with the training of Bharat took the call.

'Surya! I was about to call and you called me instead' Sudheer told checking the Jerkin. 'Did you bring the Mallu Aunty CD?' He asked intently. The shopkeeper, an old lean man with grey hair looked awkwardly at him. Sudheer frowned, gave up the jerkin and walked past to talk with solitude.

'I got a better video, Man. It seems like a horror movie. You should have been here'

'Horror movie? Don't talk like a kid. Who watch horror movies these days? You just poured water on my dreams' and he hung up the call. Surya looked with a conflicted look at the phone and resumed the video with the remote control in his hand.

The blond man slowly walked outside timidly the room to check. There was a clattering sound in the kitchen. His heart beat stopped with a sudden clanking of a steel vessel. He immediately ran down the stairs to check the kitchen. Surprisingly none was there. He nervously hyperventilated catching for breath. Sudden sound of a blast echoed in the room. Surya jumped on his seat with a shock. The man swiftly ran into the living room. The TV was turned on with a war scene going on. He didn't understand how it happened. He turned off the TV and silent walked towards the stairs. His phone rang and he shrieked and threw away the phone in horror. Surya laughed at the scene. The Caucasian took his phone and placed the receiver close to his ear. Suddenly someone grabbed from behind. He shrieked leave me. His wife answered. 'What leave me? By the way, I forgot to mention, my sister has come to our place late this night. I forgot about her coming. Take care of her'. The man became all of sudden. Now he could feel the heaving breasts clasped to his back.

'The man's eyes shone with delight. 'Don't worry dear, I will take care of her'

In the rear view of the woman, the man turned to her side with a gentle smile, he buried his face into the blonde-haired woman. Surya felt erotic with his eyes further widened. He called Sudheer. 'Macha. It's a hot scene. You missed it' kept gazing at the woman. Sudheer shouted on the other side. 'What?'

'Don't trouble. Kids shouldn't watch it' and he hung up the call with his eyes fixed to the screen.

The man carried the woman in his arms and took her to bed room. A lady slowly stripped his clothes. He pulled her black glistening dress over her hands. Surya felt excited to see her face but it was intentionally hidden to raise the curiosity in the viewers. Surya gasped for breath looking at well stuffed breasts beneath her bra with her exposed cleavage. The cameraman showed her feet and slowly elevated to her well designed translucent panty, passed the well curved beautiful waist, up to her bra. Now, the man unstrapped her lace bras revealing her well stuffed breasts. Sitting in his couch, gasping for breath, began biting his nails out of curiosity to see her face. Surya felt something familiar with the physique of the woman. The camera slowly revealed her beautiful well exposed neck, fair colored, chiseled lips and her eyes buried under her shattered blond hair

Surya suddenly stood up being flustered with confusion. A sudden wave of anguish tormented him. He couldn't believe his eyes. He paused the video and gave a closer look. He wiped his eyes out of sheer disbelief. His head spun; his legs started giving away and collapsed on the sofa being bewildered. His heartbeat increased and he perspired severely. He stood up unsteadily; removed the CD and threw away. It slid under the Bed. Ran amok to the bathroom and living room repeatedly and eventually went toward the door stumbling, raving and ranting all the way. He violently opened the door and rushed out. He happened to run into Bharat who looked baffled with his disposition. 'Are you alright Surya?' he asked. Surya took charge of his emotions and instantly transformed from an ancient man to an Egyptian doing moonwalk. He walked downstairs and headed toward his bike.

Surya banged a door. Andria stood up from the sofa in a swift movement, pivoted herself to face Surya, and confronted with a lachrymose expression. He looked so sullen and disappointed but dared not to raise an argument. He felt embarrassed. Andria looked the pain in his eyes and advanced a step to reach him Surya stood motionless and struggling to maintain his composition. His heart paced with her every

'Surya! Listen to me! Let me explain'. Surya was obviously employing herculean effort to control his disposition.

'I came to know your true colors of you. Save your energy from making futile attempts to convince me', he said meekly avoiding eye contact.

'Why don't you listen to me once before you come to a conclusion?' Andria stepped further but he repelled with one step back.

'It was my past. And you have no idea what situations demanded me to do so.', her eyes welled up with tears. It seemed to have an effect on Surya as his face had been softened a little bit but not sympathetic yet. She continued 'My mother had a heart attack. I needed money. I was all alone with none to help me then.'

Surya seemed to believe her as he chivalrously asked her to sit on the sofa. He sat beside her showing empathy. 'Sorry for that.', a gentle smile flickered on his face. 'You don't need to share anything' He said and silently sat beside her patting her back. She held her head over shoulder.

'I was in a contract with a Russian mobster to make a few videos', she said morosely. Surya consoled her. 'When I did a video, the way they had forced me to wear a scarf, and do all that.... I couldn't bear anymore. Who would care for such a hapless soul?' Andria was struggling to catch her breath out of anguish.

Surya tightened his grip on her hands. 'It's okay! You need not say anymore'.

'Let me lift off this burden' She wiped her tears. 'I felt so ashamed of what I did! When I was walking in the street, I felt like people can see me naked through my clothes! I went into depression.' Andria gasped for breath. 'That's when my cousin, the guitarist, came to my rescue. He took me with him in his band and came here to Manali to forget my past. But I don't understand how this CD came here. I saw it wrapped in a cover on your DVD player. I wondered what it could be. When I watched, I was aghast. I didn't know how to explain it to you. So, I hid it from you. Not for myself. But for you'.

Surya didn't understand how to soothe her.

'After the video was released, so many asked if I could come over for a night. You are the only one who loved me sincerely, with whom I felt safe and comfortable. I just couldn't imagine you getting hurt after knowing this truth...'.

Surya felt her words touching him so deeply that a tear drop trickled on his cheek. He gave her a hug and planted a kiss on her cheeks wiping her tears.

'I am so lucky to have you. Glad that I came to know about you'. He gently kissed her with a newly born passion. It was somewhat different than his previous sexual experience. When Raavi asked if it was love or lust, he couldn't say clearly. Now it was obvious to him what love is. He had mixed feelings of love, happiness, pain and passion which made the moment so perfect.

CHAPTER THIRTEEN

THE EAST HILL HOUSE

The other guys who went to Hampta Pass had returned from their trek. It shouldn't have taken so late to reach Manali, but the road was blocked with heavy traffic. The cab driver was a young fellow who abided strictly to the traffic rules, so, was reluctant to break the rules by jumping into another line to reach faster. All the way Sudheer and Faizaan yelled on the driver, but he put a deaf ear to them.

Surya knocked on the door, Faizaan opened it. Faizaan and Sudheer were there in the room. 'Hello Bhai! Where were you all day?' Faizaan gave him a bear hug.

Sudheer who sat cross legged on his bed said, 'Must have been with Andria. See, he was ignoring us. He was doing Andria *japam* all the time', posing a *Padmasana*. Faizaan broke into laughter. 'Seriously man! Why were you so much into that girl? What do you see in her?' Faizaan provoked him laying his hand over his shoulder. Surya countered, 'What do you see in Neha to be so much into her?' Faizaan stood silently. Sudheer laughed heavily. Faizaan gave him a grim look. He held his hand over the mouth to control his laugh, but his eyes couldn't hide it. 'How do you know that?'

'I have been watching you for a long time. You seem to have a special interest in her. Every time she comes out, your eyes shine with delight', Surya winked and continued, 'Even Sudheer explained what happened yesterday'. Faizaan gave a quick glance toward Sudheer with an angry expression. Suddenly, his expression turned soft and implored Surya, 'You have to do something Surya.

She seems to show interest in you. Anyhow, you have Andria! So, you can help us get together. She will listen to you'.

'What master plan are you cooking up in your mind?' Sudheer asked cunningly.

'Yeah. That's what! I am coming to the matter. I know a place nearby. It's a guest house of my father's friend. It had a great lake view. So...'

'So? What's in your head?' Surya asked. 'We shall go on a date there' 'You mean you and me?' Surya asked being baffled.

Sudheer looked suspiciously at his gender identity. He imagined the way Faizaan was about to kiss him. He suddenly felt nauseated.

'No! No! I mean you along with Andria and Neha... with me... if you convince her...', his voice faltered.

'OH, that's a great plan! Yeah, we shall go', Faizaan looked with an air of excitement. 'What shall I do then? Shall I do *bhajan*?!' Sudheer exploded angrily.

'Come on, *Macha*! How shall we leave you? You can join Kiran!' Faizaan broke into laughter. 'It's better if I kill myself by drowning in the lake instead of pairing up with Kiran!'

'You don't need to drown, her husband will come and drown you', Surya teased. Both of them were laughing heavily at Sudheer.

'Anyhow, let's take this hapless soul. We need a watchman there', Faizaan high-fived to Surya.

'So, mean, guys!' Sudheer contorted his face as a sign of protest.

Surya interfered, 'Okay, okay! Chill! Let's plan tomorrow'.

Faizaan interrupted, 'Huh! Surya! It's far from here. Better we start tonight so that we can reach by the daytime there'.

'Far? I heard you said nearby!' Surya looked raising one eyebrow with a questioning face. Faizaan scratched his head, 'I just said it in a flow'.

'By the way, tonight!' Sudheer exclaimed. 'Come on, Man! We didn't have proper sleep and were so exhausted yelling at the driver. Let's take good rest today'.

Surya continued, 'Yeah! That's a better idea. What do we do reach there at daytime, when all that important stuff takes place at night?' Surya grinned.

'You are awesome, *Macha*!' Faizaan gave a flying kiss to Surya. Sudheer was baffled on looking at Faizaan. 'Faizaan, we are trying so hard to set you and Neha. Don't disappoint us turning out into gay and get into our beds leaving Neha!' Sudheer pouted his mouth, imitating him so to remind him of the incident that happened the day before. Faizaan banged his head against the wall. Surya chuckled.

Sudheer asked, 'Surya what happened to the Mallu Aunty video I asked you to take yesterday night? I actually ordered and had to take myself, but I got stuck in traffic, right? So, I called you to take it. Did you?'

Surya hesitated a moment. The CD was left in Andria's room. How can he explain it was there? As the CD was taken at nighttime, it should be here at home. And Surya called back Sudheer the night before, giving assurance that he took the CD. Sudheer saw him in the morning, coming out of his room in a bad condition after watching the video. It explains that Surya was in his room all night and CD should be inside. Surya was contemplating the moment when Sudheer interrupted, 'Surya! Where is the CD?' Surya came into consciousness and blurted out, 'It was in the room'. He riveted his eyes to avoid eye contact.

'Oohhoo! We will have a great time Faizaan!' They high-fived each other.

Surya left the room and kicked the wall. 'Now I have to hide Andria's CD! No, destroy it and bring back the other CD!' He entered into his room and started looking for the CD. In the meantime, he got a call from Andria, 'Surya! I need you to be right here! Kind of an emergency'. Surya turned off the call. He rushed from the room and shut it hard from the outside. He forgot to lock the door.

Sudheer was passing by the room. He knocked at the room, 'Surya!' But didn't get any reply. He turned the knob, it was opened. He entered into the room, rotating his head studiedly. He saw a rat scurrying on the floor. He was taken aback, he looked terrified. In the flush of infuriating rage, he took a gym rod, raised his eyebrow along with his hand and said, 'I come for you! I search you! I find you and I kill you!' He laughed ferociously which looked comical. He searched for the rat under the bed and found it there. Like a Kung Fu martial artist, he did some stunts with the rod and poked it under the bed. The rat luckily escaped by an inch and ran under the sofa. Sudheer pushed the rod hard beneath the sofa which missed the rat and hit the wall with a thud sound. When he was looking for the rat, he had found a glittering object. He stood up and cursed himself, 'Shit! I missed the rat'. After a moment, out of realization, he bent again to see the glittering object.

He took it out and examined. It was a CD. He remembered that Surya had the Mallu Aunty CD. He grinned widely and with an air of excitement turned on the TV. There was no power. He took the CD with him. He thought they can watch in the resort they were planning the next day.

Surya rushed into Andria's room. 'What happened Andria? Why did you call me urgently?' Andria, being frozen with terror, looked toward Surya. 'Surya! You need to watch this'. And she showed the TV. The news was being telecasted. 'James, the guitarist, is dead!' Andria cried relentlessly. She collapsed on the floor. 'He was like a brother to me. I don't understand how it happened...!' she sobbed uncontrollably. Surya assuaged her to lessen her agony. He hugged her out of despair and terror. His hug gave her comfort. 'Do you know who did it?' Surya asked. 'I have to tell you something, Surya! Sorry, I hid something from you but didn't want to worry you'. 'What?' Surya looked baffled.

'I told you that I was in a contract with a Russian mobster.... It was not for one video but for 5 videos!' 'What!'

'Yeah! I met James in that porn industry. When I did my first film, I realized I couldn't do it anymore. James helped me to escape from there'

'Okay! What about your mother?'

'I reached my home. But somebody leaked the information that I was missing. So, they went to my home. They showed my porn video to her and threatened her'

'Then what?'

'When I reached there, she turned me away with James as it was dangerous to be there'. She took a deep breath before continuing.

'I asked her to come, but she told she wasn't fit for escaping and she would only slow us down and get us killed'.

'Is she safe now?' Surya asked out of empathy.

'After my escapade, I contacted my friend. She told me that my mother got killed', Surya was shocked! 'OMG! So, you think the Russian mobster might have done this?'

'Exactly, Surya! So, we need to escape from this place. It is no longer safe. They will kill you too!' Surya was frightened. He assured, 'Don't be frightened, Andria! I have come here to commit suicide. I don't fear about getting killed'. Andria was flustered, she did not understand what he meant. 'I am ready to die in the process of saving you'.

Tears welled up in her eyes. She came closer to him, looking into his eyes, held his head closer to hers and kissed his lips. Tears were trickling down her cheeks. 'Love you, Surya!' 'Love you too, Andria!'

'But what was that about suicide?'

'Will tell you all that later. I have a plan. My friend Faizaan's father has a friend who owns a guest house. We shall go there tomorrow. We shall stay for the night and go back to Hyderabad from there'. 'Will it work Surya? I think I will get you in trouble. Maybe it's better that I surrender' 'As long as I am alive, I can't let you do that. You are coming with me. That's it'.

Surya called Neha and told her about the plan. Neha thought for a while and accepted. He called Faizaan and Sudheer too. They finalized the plan. They called travel agencies and booked a vehicle for next day's departure.

Later, he was reminded of something and started checking her shelf. 'What?' Andria asked inquisitively. 'Mallu Aunty's porn CD!' grinned Surya. Andria raised her eyebrows and bulged out her eyes with a wide-opened mouth. Later, she clenched her teeth while repeatedly throwing fists on him playfully. 'No! No! It's for Sudheer! He is a die-hard fan of Mallu Aunty'. Andria stopped and looked at him in a moment of silence and both of them chortled into laughter.

They forgot what was to happen in the future and just enjoyed the moment. But suddenly his face puckered, his eyes almost disappeared, his breath was arrested, he took the CD from in front of his eyes, bent down and.... Aptchee!!! He sneezed. 'Bad omen', he muttered.

The next day, everyone packed their luggage and was waiting for the vehicle.

The vehicle came there on time. It was a 7-seater. Surya checked the vehicle's number. Later, he peeked into the vehicle, checked under the seats, driver's seat, and his pockets... he gave a green flag to their people with a grin as if he had triumphed in Olympics.

All of them, except Andria, looked weirdly at him. Neha nudged Surya and took the back seat saying, 'What's wrong with you Surya? You are acting weird. Don't know how many weird things I have to see'. She commented looking at Faizaan. It was obvious that she was talking about his embarrassing attempt to kiss Sudheer. Andria joined Neha trying to adjust in the small compartment. Faizaan and Sudheer occupied the 2nd row, while Surya occupied the seat beside the driver. The engine revved, rattling the vehicle. Slowly, the big vehicle took pace, smoothing the journey. The driver was driving slowly and steadily. All of them got fed up with his driving. Sudheer and Faizaan felt suspicious. They asked the driver to turn his head. The driver looked over his shoulder and greeted, 'Good morning, Sir!' He said it with a cheerful expression. Faizaan and Sudheer contorted their faces into vengeance. 'OMG! You?' they shouted in chorus. Surya asked inquisitively, 'Do you know him?' Sudheer replied with utter resentment, 'He was the one who drove us back from Hampta'.

Faizaan added, 'I plead with you! Just give your steering wheel to Surya and fuck off, man!'

It was not reprehensible to drive slowly, but to Faizaan and Sudheer, it would be a grave sin if the vehicle didn't move beyond 50 km/hr. Surya interfered, 'Come on, guys! These roads are very dangerous. You need to follow rules properly, otherwise everyone would be stuck in a traffic jam!' 'Exactly', the driver backed up Surya.

'These roads are not that comfortable as in the city. There is a speed limit'.

'Yes boss', the driver replied again in an exotic way. Surya feared if the driver would bang other vehicles in his excitement, so he ended his monologue and resolved himself to silence. Faizaan and Sudheer frowned their foreheads and twisted their mouths as a sign of protest; they started looking out through the windows.

Neha and Andria were looking at Instagram photos and giving girly giggles. They bothered about nothing, as if they were extraterrestrial aliens. Surya remembered his reference to females being an entirely different species and heaved a sigh.

Surya looked at the driver. He was young with Mongolian features with high cheekbones. He hardly looked 18. 'How he got a license? Maybe the people in this area look younger than they are, like Raavi, the 50-year-old woman who looked like she was in her 30s', Surya thought.

The car climbed hills, hit into curves, rattling all the way. The driver felt something in his nose and sneezed strongly. The vehicle lost its steady track. Everyone was shaken up and down inside. The girls came into the present world. Everyone looked aghast. But the driver simply rubbed his nose, gave a leisurely look to Surya while whistling and hissing. Surya got agitated, though he was the only person keeping cool all the time. The vehicle came to such a sudden halt that everyone was thrust forward. Surya struck his forehead on the front glass. Faizaan and Sudheer rose like zombies behind the driver to choke his neck. Surya stopped them. They disembarked the vehicle. Everyone was too exhausted. Neha started to stretch. Faizaan was drooling at her. Surya appreciated the view of the cottage. It was surrounded by a dense forest to its back and a beautiful lake harboring countless beautiful birds to its left. The driver interrupted, 'Sir! If you want to go on a long drive again... call me!' Surya was baffled. He just clasped both his hands as if he was praying. The driver giggled and went away revving his vehicle emitting a cloud of smoke from behind. All of them packed their luggage and went inside. It was a duplex cottage with an enormous hall, a kitchen and double bedroom in each floor. It looked like paradise to him. Surya comfortably sprawled on the sofa. Clock on the wall struck 5 PM.

Everyone got refreshed and lay down in the hall room. Faizaan shared his sofa with Neha while Surya shared his with Andria, facing each other. Sudheer sat in his sofa at the middle. Surya asked, 'What happened to the other guys – Chakradhar, Bharat and Kiran?'

Sudheer replied, 'Don't you know? They went to some place called Beeru near Srinagar to do paragliding'.

'Oh really?! They should have informed us. We could have joined them'.

'No man, Bharat clearly informed how dangerous these activities are! I don't want to reach my Grandmother soon'.

Faizaan interfered, 'you are frightened too much yaar; such incidents happen so rarely'.

Faizaan went upstairs all of sudden. All of them asked, 'What?' They were inquisitive.

'The name of the place Beeru reminded me of the box of beers upstairs', he replied. The eyes of Sudheer and Surya shone with enthrallment. Soon, after some time, Faizaan came back downstairs heaving a box of beers! Sudheer and Surya came to the rescue like true friends. Faizaan was surprised, 'I have never seen you guys showing so much concern, before!'

Sudheer replied with his eyes full of excitement, 'It's not for you *Macha!* It's for the beer!' focusing on the Beer box.

The trio safely landed the box with utmost care. Neha commented, 'See, they are acting as if it's their offspring born out of their threesome!' She gave a hi-five to Andria and both of them burst into giggles for some time.

They started self-serving themselves with beers. Even Andria and Neha took a bottle each. Faizaan's eyes lay on Neha; he was wondering what was written on his fate that night. He was chuckling silently. All of them hit cheers and had their first sip. Faizaan had also brought some stuff. He opened the packet and served. Andria asked Surya, 'What were you saying about suicide?'

All of them looked dumbstruck, having no idea about what she was saying. Surya felt so embarrassed that he had drunk the whole bottle of beer in one go. He thrust the empty bottle over the table among them. Everyone was looking so inquisitive about what he would say. They had their eyes wide open, gazing steadily at Surya. His chest was heaving rapidly. He started narrating his story.

'I was once doing my duty in my hospital. I was so excited with one of my interns, Prashanth'.

Sudheer almost spurted out the beer in his mouth all over Faizaan.

'Surya! You never told you are gay!'

'Listen properly, idiot. He had good respect for me and was an extrovert. On my regular duty days, I was just fixed to my duty. But that day, I was involved in conversation with the male interns'. 'It's good right? What's the problem?'

'I was talking about bodybuilding, dance, guitar and all such stuff with him. And a female intern became fascinated with me'.

'Oohhoo, Surya! You had so many girlfriends!' winked Andria.

Surya continued, 'Her name is Shravani. She started a conversation with me, it was as if I resembled to someone she knew. I prolonged the conversation'.

'Okay!' Faizaan nodded.

'She hailed from the place where I knew my relatives live. So, I showed more interest in her. We even planned to go to her home together'.

'So, what happened? Anything spicy?' Neha asked eagerly. Faizaan felt exotic when Neha talked in that way. It seemed like his trick to intoxicate her in order to get her laid was working. Faizaan was deliberately pouring more beer. He assured them not to worry after showing a full bottle Vodka. Neha brushed his cheek with her hands saying, 'Thank you dear!'

Surya continued, 'we texted each other on Instagram which seemed safe at that moment. So one day, I was texting casually. She enquired about one of the girls in my pictures who had stolen her phone'.

'OH!' everyone said in chorus.

'She asked me in frustration about why I didn't get married instead of hanging out with such girls'. Faizaan and Sudheer let their mouths fell open. 'What did you do?' Neha questioned.

'I told her that marriage would take time to occur. I just hang out with girls socially not to get desperate for anyone. IF I GET DESPERATE, YOU INTERNS WILL ONLY SUFFER. She took the statement rather seriously asking how I could say something like that. I dint know what was wrong it that. She blocked me'

'Later her boyfriend sent me vulgar messages. I took my toll upon him. In order to avenge that, she took the screenshot of my messages and showed them to the Head of the Department'.

'Oh my god! What happened?' Andria asked looking at him, grabbing his hands like a moral support. 'It was not the thing. Her mother was working as a CMO in our hospital. I reached her for some work. She talked in an involving way with me. We exchanged our numbers. While I was just having some leisure time, I texted her casually that she looks beautiful, reflecting upon her WhatsApp profile picture and courteously asked for dinner. It was just to develop good friendship with her so that she might help in my job search later'.

'So, what happened?' Andria asked with her eyes almost resembling to a bulb.

'She complained to the HOD showing the screenshot. It happened 1 month before her daughter Shravani trapped me. I realized later that the HOD was her father. The trio made a DISCO "disciplinary committee" for me. It's going to occur in 1 month. After that, I will be debarred from my college', told Surya with a frown on his face. Andria hugged him to console him. 'So, I decided to commit suicide. I just wanted to enjoy my last days happily. That's when I had seen Andria, and she changed my perspective of life', he told the last sentence while looking into Andria's eyes with his right hand grasping hers. A smile flickered on his face, she reciprocated with her own smile.

Faizaan consoled him, 'Don't worry, Surya! We will help you to get out of this. We will not let you get debarred'. Neha looked into his eyes with a smile and grasped his hand. He could sense something deep within him with her touch. She gave a peck on his cheek.

'Now I feel like getting debarred and having a pleasant life with Andria here in Manali', Surya winked at Andria who slapped his wrist playfully.

Sudheer cried deeply in the midst of them. It was not clear whether he was crying after listening to Surya's story or he was the only guy without a girlfriend. But the only thing that's clear was that he got highly intoxicated with alcohol.

'Now I have to watch this porn film. You guys are enjoying with your girlfriends; I have to enjoy with Mallu', so he opened the CD with a wicked smile.

Surya and Andria looked aghast. They realized it was Andria's CD by its mere appearance. 'It's not Mallu Aunty's CD. It's something else...', Surya rose from his sofa and grabbed the CD, pulling it toward his side.

'What's something else? Mia Khalifa?' Sudheer dragged it toward his side.

There was a war raging between them while Andria was looking anxiously, riveting her eyes toward the CD in fluttering motion. Surya was agitated, he couldn't bear Sudheer's idiocy. In a spurt of anger, he blurted out, 'It's not Mallu's CD, you idiot! It's Andria's CD!' Andria was aghast, she looked down with her hands holding her head in mental anguish. Everyone else was bewildered, especially Sudheer who had loosened his grip so that Surya could get his CD.

Everyone demanded an explanation. Surya looked at Andria regretfully and mumbled, 'Sorry'. Andria was flustered, not knowing how to react.

'Come on Surya! You can share it with us. After all, we are your friends. We can help you', Surya confusedly looked at Andria who nodded. Surya revealed everything about Andria, the Russian mobsters and James.

Faizaan was shocked as the story was too thrilling to be real. Sudheer anxiously exploded, 'So, you guys exposed me to imminent danger without me having the least idea about it! I am ready to die for friends but can't get killed without even knowing why I am getting killed!' Everyone else was puzzled whether to show sympathy or laugh at him, so all stood silent.

Everyone dispersed from the site. The clock struck 9 PM. Faizaan joined Neha for a walk in the woods. Surya went with Andria to bedroom. Sudheer ended up in his bedroom to watch Mallu Aunty's porn video. No one understood why he was so obsessed with that. Surya opened the doors of his room pleasantly and Andria walked in. Surya closed the doors behind him. Andria looked so wary, being absorbed with the thoughts of her past. Surya wondered how this girl was so steady and happy all the time despite everything she had to go through in her past. She didn't look as strong as she was before. Maybe the revelation of her past to Surya might have affected her. There was some tension between them. Surya understood her situation. In fact, he didn't want to tell anything about his past too because once if he said, it would change everything. The way people look at you, the fear of being judged crumble upon you. The HOD later informed about the incident to his parents, and his parents didn't reprimand him seriously but grounded him, his mom constantly kept nagging about the incident and asked him to be cautious. He understood that living with people who knew more about him and always in fear of being judged every time was hell. So, he didn't want to let these people know. He just wanted to live peacefully for some time. At some point of time, the truth had to be disclosed inevitably no matter how hard it was.

Surya and Andria, at present, were in such situations. Surya wanted to ease the tension. He just sat beside her gently. Andria just fell on his shoulder, laying her head over his chest and clamped her hands while looking down with a mournful smile. It seemed just like a small child hugging her mother after a dreadful nightmare. Surya patted gently on her back, held her close and brushed her hair aside over the neck. Her bosom was heaving rapidly with mixed emotions. Surya could feel her breath moving inside and gushing outside. Slowly, the rate came to normal. With a pleasant smile flickering on her face, she tilted her head toward Surya and planted a kiss on his cheek. He felt so much warmth in her company! He realized that true love was not experienced by sharing beds but when sharing thoughts, feelings and emotions.

Faizaan and Neha went outside walking step by step, enjoying their moment silently for some time on a way. Faizaan didn't know how to break the silence. Both of them were too hesitant to speak. Faizaan broke that silence, 'Neha, I want to tell a story'. 'OH, you tell stories too? Good'.

'There was an island where all feelings took residence in human form. Fear, anger, pain, love...'. 'Okay', Neha nodded with a keen interest.

'One day the island was drowning, everyone took to their boats except love, which held on to the island till the end, expecting her true love would come and help'. 'OH, I see! Poor love'.

'Love asked Greed to take her. Greed showed the wealth on his boat and said that there was no space for her'.

'Greed! It is bad', Neha told in the tone of a child.

'Love asked Sadness if it could help her. Sadness told that he was very sad and wanted to go alone'. 'So sad!' Neha smiled mournfully. 'Love asked Envy, but he was frightened that his boat might have got wrecked if he had let her step inside. She asked Anger too.... He didn't even look toward her'. 'So sorry for her!'

'Then an elder one, Knowledge, asked Love to take the boat pointing to someone. Love took that boat and reached a shore where the gentle man smiled and went away.

'Love asked the elder one when he ran into her after reaching the shore 'Who is he?'. The elder one said that he was TIME. Only time knows the value of love'.

Neha stood silently pondering about the story and asked, 'Do you think the TIME has come?'

'Yeah! Time had come and was close to you always, but you didn't recognize it yet'.

Neha took a step toward him. They locked their eyes. Faizaan entered her personal space, held her by her waist and kissed her.

CHAPTER FOURTEEN

THE MYSTERY OF THE EAST HILL HOUSE

Next day morning, Andria woke up from the bed. She pondered upon Surya's ways of sleep. She smiled slightly at him. He was in deep sleep. The moment Andria moved from her side, he involuntarily took her pillow and hugged it mumbling something indiscreetly. Andria went for a shower. By the time he woke up, he could hear the sound of the shower. He just imagined Andria naked under the shower and smiled naughtily. Later he sat for breakfast, the local housemaid prepared the meal and served them. When Surya was about to put an idli in his mouth, his phone beeped. Surya searched the content of the phone and found that it was her MMS video while she was taking a shower. He was perplexed and saw the number, but it was an unknown one. He hastily went inside the room and ran toward Andria who was drying her hair with a towel. He was flustered about how to tell her but was reluctant to tell her and checked the washroom for any hidden cameras. Nothing was found. Surya came out apprehensively and confronted Andria while violently rubbing his head. He asked her if anyone came inside. She said 'No'. He didn't understand how to reveal it to her, it would just enhance her anxiety about the Russian mobsters. He knocked on the door of Faizaan's room. Faizaan opened the door with a puzzled look, Neha was there on the bed. He gave a quick glance over Neha and returned to Faizaan. Faizaan asked 'what happened?' Surya retorted, 'Did you hear anyone coming into the room, yesterday night?' 'No... we just arrived late in the night, came straight to our room and slept. Didn't see any trespassers!'

'What happened?' Neha asked inquisitively from the back. 'Nothing... nothing..., I assume some robbery happened... as...', Surya faltered. He then added, 'Haaa... my watch was missing!' 'I never saw you wearing a watch', Faizaan wondered.

'You don't know. It was in my bag'.

'Hmmm... I have an idea! There is a CCTV camera near the door. We may find in it if anyone entered the room before Neha and I came inside last night'.

Surya's eyes shone with relief. He heaved a deep sigh, 'Let's go and check. And yeah, lock all the doors. I suspect he might be inside'. He checked every corner of the room but couldn't find anyone. Surya entered the CCTV room present in a wooden cabin outside the guest house. They opened the computer and checked for the CCTV footage between 9 PM and 10 PM. No one seemed to have walked inside. Surya was confused. He was struck with something and asked to play it again. He keenly listened to collect the details. He heard the barking of a dog. And he heard it exactly at 9.30 PM.

'Do we have any dogs?'

'Yeah, we have one in the watchman's cabin just behind. You might have noticed when we came here'. 'Yeah. So why did it bark unless it had seen someone?'

'But the CCTV shows nothing!'

'The suspect might have come through the windows!'

'But Surya, all the windows were closed and locked inside'. Neha was looking silently and keenly watching them in the cabin.

'Unless someone inside might have helped!' Neha shrugged. Surya instantly stood with a glow in his face, gave a peck on her cheek and ran inside. Faizaan and Neha exchanged looks. They followed him. Surya knocked the door of Sudheer. He opened the door with utter discomfort. 'What happened, Surya? You disturbed my dream'. Faizaan and Neha asked in unison, 'With Mallu Aunty?' Sudheer blushed with his finger under the mouth out of shyness.

Surya gave a deep sigh and regained his disposition to be strict. Surya cleared, 'Sudheer did you see anyone coming inside?' 'No, I was wasted yesterday. I slept in my room after sometime' 'Did you open the windows?' 'Haa! I felt so hot that I opened the windows for some time'. 'That's it! Sudheer opened the windows!' He looked outside through the window. It was located on the backside of the house which leads to the forest.

Neha asked, 'Why did you open it?'

'There was a power cut inside', Sudheer replied.

'But there was no power cut when we entered. Haa, I remember! There was a power cut for a few minutes. I saw the lights turn off from outside when I had a quiet walk with Faizaan', Faizaan nodded as he was reminded of the night.

'But there wasn't much power cut here. The generator turns on automatically'. Surya said, 'Let's go to the generator room'.

Everyone followed him to the room. It was seen turned off.

Faizaan asked, 'So, you think that somebody has entered the house through the window, after meddling with the generator and patiently waited for someone to open the window, which Sudheer did between 9 PM to 10 PM, just to steal your stupid watch?'

Surya succumbed to his defeat, 'Someone made MMS video of Andria while she was taking a shower'. All of them shut their mouths. Silence prevailed.

'Sorry for the mishap, Surya! But how does he know Sudheer would open the window?' 'He need not open it. The CCTV camera turns off when there is a power cut. So the suspect can directly come from the main door instead of sneaking from the window'.

'You are a genius, Surya!' Neha clapped with a smile. Faizaan interrupted, 'But the CCTV video was all well, right?'

'No, someone might have tampered with the video', he showed the video. 'See, this video is showing a copy of it in the same. Just after the dog barked, a leaf moved on the screen.... Again, after sometime, the same leaf moved on the screen. See, someone re-added the video just after the dog bark'.

'But why didn't he remove the video where the dog barked?' Faizaan questioned.

'Either he might have overlooked or left it intentionally as you guys have heard the barking sound even in the woods or the watchman might have'. 'Haa, I heard!' Neha nodded.

'See, if he tampered that, it would have been obvious that it got tampered'.

'Let's check the place outside the window.... We may get footprints of the culprit'. They checked the area. It was damp with wet mud. 'There are shoe prints!' Faizaan exclaimed. 'If he enters the house, it might have been muddy but there were no traces of mud!'

Surya cleared, 'It's pretty simple. He removed his shoes before entering. Let's call the police and forensic team for any fingerprints. And let's also get details of the owner along with his phone number'.

Faizaan called police and forensic team; it came in half an hour. They verified each and every corner of the room. Even the generator room. He took the samples of fingerprints from each and every one including Andria.

Andria asked, 'What's all this, Surya?'

Surya confidently said, 'I lost my Rolex watch'.

'You had a Rolex watch?'

'It's my friend's'.

'Who is the friend?' Surya was fed up and said, 'Andria! Everything I say in detail later. Please be silent'. 'Okay!' Andria twisted her mouth in contempt.

Forensic team head confirmed that there was no outsider's fingerprint inside the house. In the CCTV room, they found fingerprints of Faizaan, Surya and Sudheer. 'So clever! He might have used gloves to not get caught'.

Faizaan doubted, 'What about Sudheer? He didn't come into CCTV room along with us, right? How are his fingerprints present?'

Sudheer replied, 'I came here last night. Just to check the computer'.

Faizaan pondered upon something. He suddenly rushed into Sudheer's room. He checked his room. He found a pair of shoes with mud.

'See, Surya, it was him! See!'

Sudheer was shocked. Faizaan asked sternly, 'Sudheer, did you go out or not?' 'Haa, I went out to piss?!'

'Why didn't you do it inside the bathroom?'

'I was claustrophobic. It was dark inside, so I went outside'.

'Then why wasn't your video in the CCTV camera? Your fingerprints are there in CCTV room, so you might have tampered it'. Sudheer was perplexed.

Andria interfered, 'So you think that Sudheer went out to hide your Rolex watch?'

Surya said without thinking, 'What Rolex?' Then he remembered, 'Rolex watch. By the way, Andria, just go to your room. Don't take tension, we will handle things. 'Okay', Andria said and went inside.

Surya doubted, 'Why did he go outside?'

Faizaan replied, 'In order to bring the CCTV camera to fix it'.

Faizaan explained, 'It's simple. When you guys were asleep, Sudheer might have come and fixed the camera. Later, when you were having breakfast, Sudheer might have brought it out sneaking behind Andria and sent the video to his phone and sent the MMS to you. And he might have thrown away the camera in the woods'.

'No man! I didn't do anything; I didn't even use the shoe. I went barefoot. I even forgot that I have these shoes!' 'Don't try to cover the truth. You have been caught red handed'. Surya looked into Sudheer. He looked back innocently. 'Why will Sudheer does all that?'

'To blackmail you for money, Surya! Don't you remember what he did with Lydia?'

Surya nodded, 'It might be possible'. Soon, Faizaan called the police who were searching outside. They came and took Sudheer into custody. He was crying aloud 'I didn't do anything Surya'

Something about Sudheer made Surya feel that he was innocent, but his past history and evidences were against him. They clearly showed Sudheer did it. The police cuffed his hands. 'Surya! You are making a grave mistake. I am your childhood friend. Why would I do that?' Surya once again went toward the damp. He noticed something no one else did.

That evening Surya asked Sudheer who was in jail, 'Sudheer! Did you really do it?'

Sudheer nodded. 'Yes, Surya! I wanted to blackmail you and Andria so that I can have Andria for a night and extract more money from you!'

Surya shouted, 'Bastard!' And he checked the register book on the way, he looked at it for a second, wrote his name and went away.

CHAPTER FIFTEEN

THE SLOVAKIAN GIRL

Faizan was watching cricket in the Hall. Neha brought him popcorn. He was jumping on the sofa every time Kohli hit a six. Neha sat beside him asking who Lydia was. Faizaan was frozen for a second, his mouth fell open. A piece of popcorn rolled out of his hand as if some stone rolled down a hill. He slowly turned toward Neha with a baffled expression. 'Why... why are you asking Neha?' he faltered. 'Come on Faizaan, who is she?' Faizaan stood silent for a moment before starting his narration.

'Surya, Sudheer and I were good friends from school. We were all good in mathematics. Our mathematics teacher was fond of all the three of us.... We...'.

'How in the hell was that related to Lydia? Don't test my patience, Faizaan! Come straight to the point!' Neha jumped over the sofa.

'Okay, I will tell you, but I was sworn to secrecy in this issue, so don't inform Surya about this'. 'Pinky promise', Neha showed her little finger with an air of sarcasm. 'Neha!!! Don't joke! It's serious'.

'Okay, okay! Tell me what happened!'

'We went into IIT Delhi and he ended up in the medical field because of his father's force. But we kept our friendship intact. We come every year to get together.

'It happened 2 years back. Surya stayed in Hyderabad, in his rented penthouse, on the terrace away from his family. He hosted travelers to Hyderabad in his room. One of the travelers from Slovakia joined Surya's room. Sudheer and I met her in his room.

She was tall, a blondie, in her 25s, with an enigmatic appearance. Her name was Lydia. Everything about the girl was mysterious. She was so unstable – one time she was happy, and in a moment, she was angry for trivial issues. She used to take phone calls outside very secretly. So, we secretly put an eye on Lydia. Surya never cared about all that. He was just generous to her. One day Sudheer had an issue with her. That dumb fellow put his pictures along with her on dating sites, and got matches on those sites. He messaged Lydia on Instagram saying that she was a dating goddess. Lydia got so angry and put the screenshot of his message as her Instagram status. Sudheer was so hurt for being socially defamed. He put a bad review on Lydia's Facebook page. It became a big issue. Surya somehow eased the tension between them by making Sudheer apologize to Lydia. Everything seemed to be cool. Until that day...'. Faizaan was lost in thoughts. He continued, 'One day Lydia invited us for a party in Goa! We all went there in Surya's car. We were enjoying the rave party. I was taking selfies and Snapchat videos. Sudheer drank so much that he went to the bathroom and fell over there. We lifted him out and made him sit on the sofa. Surya was talking to some Mumbai girl, on the sofa, who showed keen interest on him, and her boyfriend got involved in a fight. Lydia settled the issue. Lydia sprawled on sofa after partying hard. She got a phone call and went out. Sudheer and I slowly got up from the sofa and peeked from the door left ajar. She was talking to a guy who came out of a Benz car. He wore a black suit with black specs. Lydia opened her bag and gave plenty of money to him for which he gave a small box. Later she came toward us. We went to sit on the sofa innocently. Then, Lydia sat beside us. Sudheer sat beside her and offered her some drinks. She had it and later dozed off. Sudheer stealthily took out the box from her purse. He opened it – it was a pen drive. He immediately connected it to his phone through OTG cable to see what it contained. It was her nude videos shot secretly while she was taking a shower. Surya had just arrived there and saw those videos from behind us. He slapped on Sudheer's head. "Come on, please let me copy this video", Sudheer pleaded. We said, "No".

Surya said, “We can’t let our guest be in trouble. Just put the pen drive back”. Sudheer complied half-heartedly. The next day, Lydia went away to Slovakia. What we didn’t know was, Sudheer had copied it somehow in his phone and shared it. It became viral. After a few days, we found in the news that she had committed suicide in her hometown. We realized that Sudheer was the reason for all that. We reprimanded him. He felt sorry and attempted suicide when we didn’t talk to him. So, we eased the tension by forgiving him. Once even the police came, but we managed somehow. We told them the video might have been leaked by the blackmailers even after taking their ransom without abiding to their deal’.

Neha was perplexed with her mouth wide opened and eyes bulged out. She sat back to normal posture with her elbows over her knees, semi-flexed, and hands under her head. ‘What have you done guys? You have killed a girl!’

‘That’s not my idea to copy or leak the video. The burden was totally on Sudheer’. ‘But you helped him to get the pen drive, right?’

‘Yeah, I did that out of curiosity! If I had known that it would lead to such things, I wouldn’t have done that!’ Faizaan retorted strongly.

‘Okay! Whatever had happened just happened. I think, someone, maybe some relatives of Lydia, might have trapped Sudheer now’.

‘You are thinking too much. It’s real life, not reel life. I am damn sure that it was all because of his bad habit of voyeurism. Now, he was tempted to take Andria’s video as well! Asshole! Because of him, we had to suffer’.

CHAPTER SIXTEEN

THE RIDE TO DELHI

Surya wore a jerkin of Harley Davidson, wore its iconic Helmet and sat on a Harley Davidson. He went on a lonely road which hit so many curves on the way to reach the city of Delhi. He went into an Airtel showroom. He told the receptionist, 'I want the details of a phone number'. He showed a number from which he got the MMS video. She was reluctant to do so, 'Sorry sir, it is against the rules to disclose the information of our customers'. He came closer to her and said, 'I got an MMS video from this number. It's a sensitive issue. I want to know the information. Please'.

She looked cautiously all over the room, after ensuring that no one was looking at her, she said, 'Okay, sir! Give me your number, I will send you the details'.

'Thank you'. He scribbled some numbers on a piece of paper and gave it to her. She stealthily took it.

When Surya came out of the showroom, riding his way back to Manali, he got a message. It was the details of the customer. He went to the address. It was from Delhi. It was taken on a girl's name, Harshaja Gupta. He went to the address. He opened the gate and pressed the calling bell. A girl in her 30s, fair skinned, wearing kurta pajama opened the door. 'Yes!' 'Is this Harshaja Gupta?'

'Haa, yes! I am. Tell me?'

'Is this your number?' he showed her the number.

'Yeah, it was. But it is no longer used by me'.

'Why?' 'A foreign girl who I hosted a few months back had that SIM for domestic use', she added. 'So, you didn't block it later?'

Surya asked.

'No, I didn't. Why would I have to? She looked trustworthy'.

'Because if someone commits a crime using that number, you will be in trouble!' 'What happened?' she asked being perplexed.

'I got an MMS of nude videos of my girlfriend from that number', Surya retorted sternly with harsh tone.

The girl was dumbstruck. 'I never knew such things happen!' 'Where was she from? How does she look like?'

'She looked blonde, tall, and slim, with long legs. Surya felt helpless with the information. Because most foreigners look tall and blonde.

'What was her name?'

'I don't know her real name, but she introduced herself as Lydia from Slovakia'

Surya pondered over the details. 'How could it be possible? Lydia was dead 1 and half year ago! How on earth did she land in Delhi? I saw myself on TV, the footage of her committing suicide by falling from her college building', Surya was obsessed with her. He even gave a thought if it was something supernatural, though it was hard to believe. 'So many stupid unbelievable things are happening these days, why can't the existence of souls be one of it?'

He came back to the room; Andria was so angry with him that he left without saying anything.

'What happened, Surya? Where did you go?' Andria confronted him seriously.

'It's nothing, Andria! I had to visit a relative in Delhi. I went to meet him'.

'Hmmm, it's okay'. He was frustrated and felt guilty for hiding things from Andria. But he seemed to have no other alternative. He just kissed her cheeks and went out.

CHAPTER SEVENTEEN

VERSIONS OF TRUTH

One day Surya's senior caught Surya in the restroom instead of being at his work. His senior gave him a lecture. Surya had his own reasons for being there. He was jotting up some lines for a novel. Anyhow, there were no new cases in Surgical Emergency ward, so he just wanted to use some time productively on his novel. According to Surya, he was doing right, but for the senior he was just escaping from work.

Surya was sitting near the balcony on an armchair and was pondering upon this incident that happened in the hospital. He alluded it to Sudheer. 'What if Sudheer was doing something right, but we are thinking all wrong?' 'What if Sudheer was protecting someone?' 'If Sudheer is innocent, who could have done this?' He found alibis for everyone. Neha and Faizaan were out for a quiet walk. They went away and came back at 10 PM. The watchman was the witness who saw them walking toward the front of the house. The housemaid didn't come on that day and she, usually, leaves by afternoon. The watchman didn't even enter the house as there were no fingerprints of him; he is in his 50s – old and shrunken. Surya couldn't imagine him doing it. And there was no reason.

As Surya was deeply contemplating about the recent events, Andria appeared from behind and clamped her arms across Surya. Surya felt relief in her touch. She came to the front and sat across him. 'So what were you thinking so much about?' she asked being concerned. 'Andria! I am so stressed with the recent events. I just want to escape from this place' 'All this for Rolex watch? Hmmm...!'

Surya felt guilty whether to say it or not.

He continued, 'Why don't we go to Old Manali?'

'Surya, I am too frightened by the place. Do you really think that's a great idea?' 'Yeah, definitely! Those are memories right?' Surya said pulling her cheeks.

They started their journey on his Harley Davidson bike. They had retraced the path, hit curves and hills, and finally reached Manali by that night. They reached the Elite House. They entered the hall room with giant sofas and giant windows. Surya rested there for a while and leisurely looked at the view through the window.

'You just relax, Surya! I will have a shower'.

'Yeah, sure!' Surya scrutinized her room. Andria was humming songs while she was in the shower. Surya went toward the TV and went through the CDs. He watched something and he turned the TV off after getting bored. He walked toward her make-up kit. There was a box, hair dye and a comb. He just casually went through them. There was nothing so striking to him. Andria came out of her shower in a towel, she nudged Surya out of her bedroom playfully so that she can dress. Surya was pleading with her to let him stay with a wicked smile. She told 'No!' with pretended anger and closed the bedroom door. He was waiting in the hall room. It was already 9 PM in the night. Next day, they went out for river rafting; they were drenched with the water of Beas River. They climbed Rohtang Pass, played with snow while wearing thermals, did paragliding and touched the limits of the sky. They had a great time together. Surya had some kind of Peter tingling (Spider sense) – that somcthing bad was going to happen – so he rejoiced the time he had with Andria.

Chapter 18
THE BLACKMAILER

T

he next day, they returned back early in the morning to reach East Hill House. After reaching the house, he headed to the prison and came back by the evening.

When he was parking his bike, he got a message. It was again the video of Andria taking a shower. The threat wasn't over with the arrest of Sudheer. He got a phone call from the same number. Surya picked up the call, 'Hello?'

'If you don't want this video to go viral, I want you to follow my orders exactly'. It was obvious that his voice was modified using technology.

'NO! Don't do that! I will exactly do what you say!' Surya's voice quivered.

'Good! I want you to arrange 1 million as ransom'.

'1 million!? Okay, I will arrange for it'.

'I will call you once the money has been arranged'.

He made a few phone calls to his Aunt who was a veterinarian doctor and got the money transferred to his account. He rode his bike to a nearby bank. He came back with a suitcase. He sent the picture of the money, in a suitcase, to the blackmailer. After a few minutes, he got a call again.

'Good! Now, go inside and bring Andria to the back of the house, into the woods'. 'What!' Surya was dreaded. 'You only want the money, right? Why do you want to involve Andria?' 'Just do as I say! Otherwise, this video leaks!'

Surya tried being smart, 'Why do I have to worry! There is a porn video of her, already. Does it really matter if you make it viral?' There was silence.

'Surya! Didn't Andria ever say that she destroyed the videos on her escapade from the Russian mobsters? She had only one CD which she took away to rat out the Russian mobsters to the police'. Surya pondered for some time, 'How did he know that Russian mobsters did the porn video? He didn't say anything about that to Sudheer. It's clearly not Sudheer or any of his mates'. Surya regretted, 'I busted him. I didn't even believe my school friend. Cha...!' 'Surya! Listening? Do what I say!'

Surya wondered what would happen if he was the Russian mobster. If he takes Andria, definitely they would abduct her and draw her into the porn industry. Surya took the risk! 'Yeah, I will bring her too'.

Later, Surya made some phone calls to his parents and his friends. It could be his end. Because what he was going to do would risk his life. He went into the kitchen and took a knife along with him and went to the back of the house, into the woods. There were clearly arrow marks on the path with white color which lead to another path. The symbols were glistening as if made out of some radium paint. Surya followed the paint alone without Andria. After walking a few kilometers, there was a "right turn", and later a "left turn". He went through the dense forest, shoving away the branches of the trees from the way, taking the ragged path slowly, being aware of the rocks. He could hear large splashing sounds as if there was a waterfall ahead. There were sounds of some animals scurrying at a distance – might have been a rabbit. There was also the howling of a wolf! Surya was anxious with sweat coming out of his body. He was frightened. So he relaxed himself, breathing deeply, saying a mantra "The Sun, the Moon and the Truth" a Buddhist Mantra he learnt when he went to the Himalayas. He had a bag in which he put all his money. After some distance, he noticed a tall guy with a hood was standing facing the other direction.

'So, Surya! Finally, you reached! Did you bring the Money?'

His voice was muffled, might have used some instrument, with a Russian accent. Surya was confirmed that it was a Russian mobster. Silhouette of the person seemed to be well-known.

'Why do I have a feeling that you have come alone?' The blackmailer turned toward his side. He had a hood which was carved on two sides to allow the eyes to be visible – they were blue in color with a high eyebrow line. 'Where is Andria?'

'See, let's not involve Andria in this. You can have all the money you want'.

'Surya! What a love! How could you love such a bitch who would sleep and make a video for money?'

Surya clenched his hands into a hard fist, trying to control his anger. 'Let's have the deal! Take the money and leave!!!'

'But it's too late Surya!'

He heard the sound of someone coming from behind. Surya turned his head mumbling.

'Andria?'

'Surya!'

'I had called her too and said that I kidnapped you', said the blackmailer with a sinister laugh. 'Andria! You should have called me, right... before coming here?'

'I was so worried and rushed. Anyhow, how can I leave you here alone!?'

'What a lovely couple! I regret so bad that it has to end this way!' he took out a gun from his outfit. Surya and Andria were terrified.

'Now, Andria, come to this side with the money or else I will shoot Surya!'

Andria complied with the blackmailer and went beside him. He put a hood on Andria and pointed the gun at Surya.

Andria was shouting, 'No! Don't do anything to Surya!'

'Kneel down and put your hands up, Surya'.

He complied with him.

'I feel sorry, Surya that I have to kill you!'

Surya laughed! The blackmailer and Andria were puzzled.

Surya continued, 'Don't you want to check if it is the original currency?'

Blackmailer turned his head being distracted. Surya took out the knife he hid in his socks swiftly and threw it at his right hand which was holding the gun. It pierced his palm and the gun fell from his hand somewhere. He hinted Andria to run away and he ran toward the kidnapper and blew fists hard at his face. Someone shouted, 'Stop!' She was pointing the gun at Surya!

It was Andria! 'Andria what are you doing?' 'Sorry, Surya! I don't think I have any option', Andria said with a sinister look.

Surya kneeled down with his hands up.

'That is a Beretta M9, right?'

'So, you know about guns too?'

'Do you know what? We doctors follow a rule – shake well before use! Seems like you didn't check the gun before using.'

'What are you saying?'

Faizaan, Neha and the police officers who were hiding in the place came out. Surya stood up and took the gun out of her hand. Andria was bewildered. She was a professional shooter, but the spark and confidence in Surya paralyzed her.

He gently took the revolver. The blackmailer who was trying to run was stopped by the police ACP Samar with his gun. 'Situation under control', said the police.

Faizaan said in utter confusion 'Surya! You said that Andria was the culprit! How could you deduce that? And who is that blackmailer?'

Surya went toward the blackmailer who was kneeling down with hands up.

'It's none other than James!' he said and removed the hood.

James was looking at everyone with bewilderment.

He turned out his pockets, 'It's the missing phone he used to take her video'.

Everyone was in shock! They had no clue about what was happening.

CHAPTER EIGHTEEN

THE BLACKMAILER

The next day, they returned back early in the morning to reach East Hill House. After reaching the house, he headed to the prison and came back by the evening.

When he was parking his bike, he got a message. It was again the video of Andria taking a shower. The threat wasn't over with the arrest of Sudheer. He got a phone call from the same number. Surya picked up the call, 'Hello?'

'If you don't want this video to go viral, I want you to follow my orders exactly'. It was obvious that his voice was modified using technology.

'NO! Don't do that! I will exactly do what you say!' Surya's voice quivered.

'Good! I want you to arrange 1 million as ransom'.

'1 million!? Okay, I will arrange for it'.

'I will call you once the money has been arranged'.

He made a few phone calls to his Aunt who was a veterinarian doctor and got the money transferred to his account. He rode his bike to a nearby bank. He came back with a suitcase. He sent the picture of the money, in a suitcase, to the blackmailer. After a few minutes, he got a call again.

'Good! Now, go inside and bring Andria to the back of the house, into the woods'. 'What!' Surya was dreaded. 'You only want the money, right? Why do you want to involve Andria?' 'Just do as I say! Otherwise, this video leaks!'

Surya tried being smart, 'Why do I have to worry! There is a porn video of her, already. Does it really matter if you make it viral?' There was silence.

'Surya! Didn't Andria ever say that she destroyed the videos on her escapade from the Russian mobsters? She had only one CD which she took away to rat out the Russian mobsters to the police'. Surya pondered for some time, 'How did he know that Russian mobsters did the porn video? He didn't say anything about that to Sudheer. It's clearly not Sudheer or any of his mates'. Surya regretted, 'I busted him. I didn't even believe my school friend. Cha...!' 'Surya! Listening? Do what I say!'

Surya wondered what would happen if he was the Russian mobster. If he takes Andria, definitely they would abduct her and draw her into the porn industry. Surya took the risk! 'Yeah, I will bring her too'.

Later, Surya made some phone calls to his parents and his friends. It could be his end. Because what he was going to do would risk his life. He went into the kitchen and took a knife along with him and went to the back of the house, into the woods. There were clearly arrow marks on the path with white color which lead to another path. The symbols were glistening as if made out of some radium paint. Surya followed the paint alone without Andria. After walking a few kilometers, there was a "right turn", and later a "left turn". He went through the dense forest, shoving away the branches of the trees from the way, taking the ragged path slowly, being aware of the rocks. He could hear large splashing sounds as if there was a waterfall ahead. There were sounds of some animals scurrying at a distance might have been a rabbit. There was also the howling of a wolf! Surya was anxious with sweat coming out of his body. He was frightened. So he relaxed himself, breathing deeply, saying a mantra "The Sun, the Moon and the Truth" a Buddhist Mantra he learnt when he went to the Himalayas. He had a bag in which he put all his money. After some distance, he noticed a tall guy with a hood was standing facing the other direction.

'So, Surya! Finally, you reached! Did you bring the Money?'

His voice was muffled, might have used some instrument, with a Russian accent. Surya was confirmed that it was a Russian mobster. Silhouette of the person seemed to be well-known.

'Why do I have a feeling that you have come alone?' The blackmailer turned toward his side. He had a hood which was carved on two sides to allow the eyes to be visible – they were blue in color with a high eyebrow line. 'Where is Andria?'

'See, let's not involve Andria in this. You can have all the money you want'.

'Surya! What a love! How could you love such a bitch who would sleep and make a video for money?'

Surya clenched his hands into a hard fist, trying to control his anger. 'Let's have the deal! Take the money and leave!!!'

'But it's too late Surya!'

He heard the sound of someone coming from behind. Surya turned his head mumbling.

'Andria?'

'Surya!'

'I had called her too and said that I kidnapped you', said the blackmailer with a sinister laugh. 'Andria! You should have called me, right... before coming here?'

'I was so worried and rushed. Anyhow, how can I leave you here alone!?'

'What a lovely couple! I regret so bad that it has to end this way!' he took out a gun from his outfit. Surya and Andria were terrified.

'Now, Andria, come to this side with the money or else I will shoot Surya!'

Andria complied with the blackmailer and went beside him. He put a hood on Andria and pointed the gun at Surya.

Andria was shouting, 'No! Don't do anything to Surya!'

'Kneel down and put your hands up, Surya'.

He complied with him.

'I feel sorry, Surya that I have to kill you!'

Surya laughed! The blackmailer and Andria were puzzled.

Surya continued, 'Don't you want to check if it is the original currency?'

Blackmailer turned his head being distracted. Surya took out the knife he hid in his socks swiftly and threw it at his right hand which was holding the gun. It pierced his palm and the gun fell from his hand somewhere. He hinted Andria to run away and he ran toward the kidnapper and blew fists hard at his face. Someone shouted, 'Stop!' She was pointing the gun at Surya!

It was Andria! 'Andria what are you doing?' 'Sorry, Surya! I don't think I have any option', Andria said with a sinister look.

Surya kneeled down with his hands up.

'That is a Beretta M9, right?'

'So, you know about guns too?'

'Do you know what? We doctors follow a rule – shake well before use! Seems like you didn't check the gun before using.'

'What are you saying?'

Faizaan, Neha and the police officers who were hiding in the place came out. Surya stood up and took the gun out of her hand. Andria was bewildered. She was a professional shooter, but the spark and confidence in Surya paralyzed her.

He gently took the revolver. The blackmailer who was trying to run was stopped by the police ACP Samar with his gun. 'Situation under control', said the police.

Faizaan said in utter confusion 'Surya! You said that Andria was the culprit! How could you deduce that? And who is that blackmailer?'

Surya went toward the blackmailer who was kneeling down with hands up.

'It's none other than James!' he said and removed the hood.

James was looking at everyone with bewilderment.

He turned out his pockets, 'It's the missing phone he used to take her video'.

Everyone was in shock! They had no clue about what was happening.

CHAPTER NINETEEN

SOLVED MYSTERY

Surya took all of his team and showed the damp area. Faizaan and Neha followed him. 'What do you observe?' Surya questioned. Both of them looked keenly and Faizaan said, 'Two pairs of shoeprints'. 'And?' asked Surya.

'One's going toward the house and another is going into the woods', Neha told observing keenly. 'What else do you observe?'

Both of them remained silent for a moment, pondering upon the scene. Then Faizaan replied, 'Yeah, Surya! One pair of shoe prints is deep while the others are superficial'. 'What does it imply?' Surya asked inquisitively.

Neha contemplated about that and said, 'I remember the day we came here, there was rain. It was all wet! If the person who passed at that time had deep shoe prints, and... he might have left after some time... indeed that must have been a long time as all the damp is almost dry. It was when this second pair of shoe tracks was left... more superficial to former'.

'Exactly!' Surya replied with a spark in his eyes. 'The culprit, I mean James, stayed for the whole night in the cold weather'.

'How do you know he was outside? Why didn't he come in?'

Surya led them a little closer toward the backside of East Hill House toward lake-side view. 'See, the shoe prints end here. He didn't pass beyond it. So, whatever he had done, it related to Andria, showing the window on the 2nd floor. We took that room because we wanted a lake-side view'.

He later took them to the CCTV footage room. He opened the footage video. 'We have Sudheer's fingerprints here in this which made us believe that he was the culprit. But he just went out to pee and played with this computer being drunk' 'Okay!' nodded Faizaan& Neha.

'But there is something more interesting about this video'. And he showed another CCTV footage.

Faizaan and Surya stooped over the monitor. It's the CCTV camera on the front gate. He particularly showed a snippet of the video, zoomed it and showed to Faizaan! Faizaan looked at the man, in his early 30s with a beard, tall and well-built with bulged biceps and wearing an old shirt. He looked like the woodcutter as he held a saw in his hands.

'What do you infer from this?'

'Facial features are not clear.... Wait a minute! What's that?' He pointed out the finger on his left arm. There was an eagle tattoo with a cross in its heart.

Surya explained, 'It's the Slovak Eagle tattoo. Do you remember where you have seen it before?'

Faizaan pondered upon it, 'Yeah! The night we came to Manali.... On the guitarist, yeah, James!!!' Faizaan looked at the time the video was captured. 'So, it was captured at 1 PM; the day before we came here', Faizaan looked astonished.

'Exactly! And there was no exit. So, he was staying in the woods since then. And this tattoo explains his Slovakian connection. Do you remember who else was from Slovakia?'

Faizaan thought for a minute and exclaimed, 'Lydia! So, you think there is a connection with Lydia?'

'I wanted to find any clues through which I could link Andria, Lydia and James. So, I headed to Andria's residence, the Elite House. And I even remember someone named Lydia in Delhi, at Harshaja Gupta's residence'.

Faizaan stood erect with shock, 'I thought Lydia was dead. You know we watched it in the news!' He shrugged.

'Let's go to Elite House. You will be surprised with what I have found there'. They went to the Elite House and entered the hall room. Surya led Faizaan toward a mirror in the bedroom. There was a rack in it. Surya held the knob and drew it back. There was a dark box that he held over Faizaan's left hand. He opened it to show Faizaan. Faizaan saw a pair of blue contact lens wrapped inside.

He opened another rack; there he showed a black dye. Surya held it over Neha's right hand. Both of them exchanged looks. 'What's this?' Neha asked inquisitively with her eyes wide open. 'I told you, I went to Delhi tracking the address of the number I got the message from'. Faizaan and Neha nodded.

'The SIM was in the name of Harshaja Gupta who gave her it to a Slovakian girl, a few months back. She described the girl was tall and blonde with blue eyes!'

'I am not getting you', Faizaan was confused.

'Lydia was dead 1 and half year back. I was shocked to hear that she stayed in Delhi. But when I saw this, I was confirmed. Andria used these lenses to stay as Lydia there. And this dye to hide her blonde hair. She, in fact, had blonde hair'.

'Really? How do you know that?'

He was scrounging through her clothes in her shelf looking particularly for something. Then he removed a picture under her clothes. It showed a guy standing in the center. He was lean and tall, with grey hair, holding two blonde girls on either side. 'See, this black-eyed blonde is Andria; to the right of the guy, it's her old pic which she took when she was near 15'.

'What about the other guys?' Neha pointed out.

'The other blondie with blue eyes was Lydia? And this guy...'.

Faizaan interrupted, 'James, I can see the Slovakian Eagle'.

'Exactly!!!'

Faizaan asked, 'Surya! Andria told James was dead, right?'

'Yeah, even I believed that initially until I saw this CD', Surya played the CD. It's the same video he watched before the day of his arrival to the East Hill House. 'What! So... was it made-up story that James was dead? But why?'

'To instill fear of the Russian mobsters in me, so that I take her to the East Hill House where she can exhibit her plan'.

'But Surya, it was my idea to go to The East Hill House!' 'Really? Try to remember, did she influence you in anyway?'

Faizaan pondered upon it, 'Yeah, I remember her talking about the place casually on the night of concert and a few times later describing about the beauty. When I inquired about it I had realized that it was a property of my father's friend'. 'See, she mentally toyed with you to choose this place and later she planned all she wanted'.

'Okay! Sudheer confessed everything, how do you explain that?'

'Yeah, I got the doubt when I observed the shoe prints. So, I approached Sudheer to find what happened that evening. But he refused to say and he confessed to the crime', Surya took a deep breath. 'While I was leaving, I observed something'. 'What?' Neha asked inquisitively. She was biting her nails.

'It's better that I show you'. They went to the prison in which Sudheer was incarcerated. 'At the reception, everyone who meets him has to write their name'.

He showed the register. Faizaan and Neha stooped to see it. Neha was shocked to see it because someone had written Nazma!

'How Surya?! Nazma left for Hyderabad a few days back!' 'Yeah, I know. So, I asked the jailer. He said someone came in a burqa to see him. She had said that her name was Nazma, she wore spectacles'.

'Nazma doesn't wear spectacles'.

'I asked him what he had observed.... He told that, accidentally, the hood on her head fell aside because of the wind and he could see boy-cut hair'. 'Kiran!' Faizaan and Neha shouted.

'To confirm that I met Sudheer, he told that someone in Burqa blackmailed him by showing his sex video with his boss' wife, and to confess to the crime'.

Neha doubted, 'He should have recognized the voice'.

He told that she didn't even talk to him. Just signed in sign language.

'How did Sudheer know sign language?' Neha doubted.

'He had to. Because his sister was deaf and dumb'.

Surya continued, 'Sudheer also said that he was the one who anonymously sent me Andria's porn CD to break our relationship. He got suspicious about her and followed her to her home. He didn't know about Lydia's connection and all, but all he sensed was that the girl would be a trouble. Later he found the CD in the old Manali shop which Andria put intentionally, which I came to know when I inquired the old man. She told him to give it to a thin lean spectacled guy at right time. But he accidentally gave him earlier which was sent in courier before Andria could develop a strong relationship. So she hid until the right time came to instill fear of the Russian Mobsters without breaking my trust on her.'

Later, Surya put a round-table conference at home. ACP Samar was also there.

'The two reasons which are making Sudheer innocent are....

First, the shoe prints. Behind the house, at the entry into the woods, there was damp soil, you remember? The shoe prints were present on two ways – one way was toward the house and another away from the house. Both the trails were lost in the woods and near the house. But one thing peculiar about these trails was, the set of shoe prints toward house was deep, while the one away from the house was slightly superficial. It seems there was a huge time gap. Before the day of the incident it rained, so it was wet, footprints were deep. That person might have stayed outside all night for some reason and went away the next morning when the slightly superficial prints were imprinted. To tolerate such cold, he might have been physically fit... in fact, extraordinarily fit'.

Faizaan interrupted, 'So, he was James, right? Why did he want all night?'

'To take the missing mobile of Lydia in which Andria's video of showering was stored...'. Surya showed the phone as he turned out his pocket, 'How would he do that without coming inside? There were no fingerprints of him anywhere inside. Someone might have helped from inside to take the phone. He could simply throw it over so that the other person from the window might have caught it. Who was the person that caught the phone from the window? Let's think Faizaan or Neha. The one who helped to catch the phone might have tampered with the video and generator. As Faizaan and Neha went on a walk, they couldn't have tampered with the generator and CCTV footage. Watchman was the strong witness. And James foot prints ended near the wall and didn't reach the generator or CCTV room. It's Andria who opted out. She helped James'.

'Sudheer might have helped, but the connection with Lydia's phone wasn't comprehensible. Why would Sudheer get Lydia's phone and do all this and send out to a stranger? Why would he give the outsider his shoes so that his footprints could be tracked?' Faizaan and Neha nodded in agreement.

'When I went to meet Sudheer after his arrest... however, that was my plan with ACP Samar. He earnestly accepted to help me distract the real criminal'. Surya turned toward him and said, 'Thank you, sir!'

ACP Samar nodded with a smile, 'It's my pleasure'.

Surya continued, 'Some person entered to see Sudheer. There was some Nazma in the register. Definitely, it was fake. When I asked the jailer, he said that a girl wearing burqa went to meet Sudheer. She might have used something to blackmail Sudheer'.

Surya specifically focused on Faizaan.

'Sudheer had some affairs in the past with the wife of his boss. What if she secretly used to blackmail Sudheer and made him confess to the guilt?'

Faizaan nodded, 'Yeah. There might be a chance'. Surya approached him the next day and explained all his doubts. Sudheer confessed that someone was blackmailing him but didn't reveal the name as he didn't know who it was. He was just told to accept the crime or the video would become viral. And he also said that he was the one who sent Surya the porn CD of Andria, which he accidentally found in the Old Manali shop. He sent to show that he could break their relationship.

'That was Kiran, right? The woman who came in burqa?' Neha nodded.

'But I needed more evidence to establish connection Kiran, Andria and Lydia. So, I planned a trip with Andria to her residence – Elite House. I found strong evidence there when I was spending time leisurely with her. I looked for one thing which can clear everything. That was a CD. When Andria went to the washroom, I watched the CD. It was made up news that James was dead'.

'Why she had to do that?'

'Because Andria was so intelligent. She terrified me and made this plan to the East Hill House where she could implement her plan to trap Sudheer.

'She knew about the place very well as she had been here for months and it was the perfect place to implement the plan. So, she supported me or else she might have chosen her own place of interest'.

'Why did she do that? All for the ransom?' Neha asked.

Surya replied, 'It's not just for the ransom money. I wanted to verify what the reason was. In Andria's room, I just didn't find the CD. I found three more items. One was dye used to color her hair. In fact, Andria was a blonde, which I found out later. Another item was her eye lens, which were blue, to disguise as Lydia while she stayed for few months as Lydia. And the Beretta M9, which was fully loaded. I emptied it the night before the blackmail'.

Surya continued, 'She stayed at Harshaja Gupta's residence in the name of Lydia. That's when she did all the groundwork about Surya and his friends'.

Faizaan questioned, 'How did she know our details? That we were coming to Manali, when and where we were staying, all that?'

'There was a black sheep in our gang. She was none other than Kiran. I checked Andria's phone and I found that there were so many calls between Kiran and Andria. Kiran was a cousin of Shravani – my subordinate'.

Faizaan raised his eyebrows.

Surya looked, 'Yeah, you know Shravani, right?'

Neha answered, 'Yeah, I remember. You told about her; other CMO mom, HOD father when we were at the East Hill House. Very funny story', she chuckled.

Surya gave a stern look for which Neha became alert.

'She misinterpreted that I harassed her sister and behaved badly with her aunt. Kiran wanted to take revenge on me. She joined Andria who came to know about her when she did her groundwork on me. Kiran found that I was interested in trekking, so she intentionally joined the trekking group planned to Manali. She gave Andria every update about me. Andria informed James and both planned to come to Manali from Delhi and Slovakia respectively. They shifted to Manali a few weeks before I planned the trip. James and Andria were cousins of Lydia'.

Neha interfered, 'Yeah, Lydia! Faizaan told about her story. How she committed suicide when her nude video got leaked. So Andria took revenge behalf of her cousin'.

Surya stared at Faizaan for leaking the information, he shrugged.

Neha asked, 'How did they plan all this in this East Hill House? Any explanation Mr. Neighborhood detective?'

Surya smiled and continued, 'James was waiting there in the woods all night for Andria's signal. Andria gave flickering light as signal to proceed when she ensured that I was past asleep. She added sleeping pills to the milk I drank. Next moment, she threw Sudheer's shoes from her window, which was toward the lake, in tangential direction into the woods.... I intentionally chose the room so that we could enjoy the lake view'.

Surya gave a deep sigh. He continued, 'She was athletic, a champion of javelin throw. I remember seeing Andria in one of Lydia's albums of her family photos, which was shot long back. It was Lydia with her young cousin – blonde with black eyes, who might be in her 15 in the picture – holding a Victory cup in her hands. So, she could have thrown the shoes, which were stolen from Sudheer, into the woods easily. James wore the shoes and entered near the window and threw the phone in which Harshaja Gupta's SIM was inserted. She caught it accurately. James, one of the cousins of Lydia, himself was an athlete and could easily throw the phone. He was the guy whose picture Lydia showed; she said she used to kiss him on the lips when she was young, pointing to a teenage kid's picture. Andria caught the phone and put with her all night. One of the dogs saw him and barked at him. He threw a biscuit which had sedative in it. The dog ate it and slept. James stayed outside all night in such cold. His determination to take revenge was seen in that. He saw Faizaan and Neha coming through the front gate. He carefully hid. The next morning, when Andria went to shower, she recorded her nude video in that bathroom and threw it to James. James caught the phone. James went out through the damp into the woods. The damp soil was dried to some extent by the time. So that's why the foot tracks were superficial. Here, the athletic skills of both people were so evident. James threw the shoe exactly over the window and she might have caught it'.

Faizaan interfered, 'I think you are exaggerating about Andria as she was your girlfriend'.

Surya explained, 'Let's imagine Andria might have worn gloves which we had bought for the Rohtang Pass trek, and went out and gave the shoes at night. Then she might have got recorded in CCTV but not. But if this had happened, James would have left at night. And the cellphone should have been inside with Andria, but we found it in James's pocket now. I was sitting in the hall while having breakfast, so there's no way she could have gone down to hand it over to him without being caught'.

Faizaan nodded with a smile of agreement. 'So, James stayed up all night to collect the phone with MMS video. Who turned off the generators to make Sudheer come out to get into the trap? Andria, right? As there were no footprints or fingerprints of James near the generator... while Andria wore gloves... even if she was caught with her footprints, she could say that she went casually over there'.

Surya answered, 'Exactly! She turned off the generator at night and the next morning, she woke up before me, wore the gloves and tampered with the CCTV footage too to delete her video along with Sudheer's, so even if others found out the video was tampered, they would have doubt on Sudheer as his fingerprints were present. What a genius! And James later went away into the woods, from where he used his athletic skills to throw his shoes. What a stunt! It was not easy either to throw or to catch'.

Samar interrupted, 'But how were you sure that it was James? The made-up CD you found out in Elite House just ensures he was alive'. He looked inquisitively.

Surya showed a snippet of CCTV footage. 'Even a great criminal makes small mistakes. There was a CCTV camera near the gate too. James was recorded there at 1 PM in the disguise of a carpenter....

Andria messaged him about the location and immediately deleted it. James came in the disguise of a Carpenter to cut trees in the forest. And he stayed for a long time because there was no video showing him exit. There was a tattoo on his left arm – Slovakian Eagle symbol. I remember it from the day of the concert'.

Everyone else nodded.

CHAPTER TWENTY

THE TRUE VERSION OF TRUTH

Andria was sitting in the custody with her hands on her forehead, with her head held low and deeply contemplating about what would happen. Suddenly, the door creaked. Surya came inside. The room was secured with a CCTV camera and voice recorder. There was a large window which was transparent from inside, as seen in regular old-fashioned movies. On the other side Faizaan, Neha and Samar were looking sternly and focused, thinking about what she would say.

Surya warmed up before this. He even did rehearsals in front of the mirror. It was so difficult for him to take charge of his emotions while trying to find out the Truth. Samar wanted to take the proceedings in his own hand, but Surya interfered, he knew more about Andria, so it was better he dealt with it.

Surya took his seat opposite Andria, looking into her eyes for a minute. 'So, what do you say about all this Andria? Do you accept the crime?'

'What was the crime I did anyway?'

'You recorded your own video and made Sudheer suffer for this'.

'See, I didn't even know what was going on then. You said you had lost your Rolex watch and you people came to conclusions'.

'Okay! What about the blackmail from James?'

'Yeah! It came from his side. He blackmailed you. So, he was the culprit, how could I be? Is there any proof to establish the connection between us?'

He showed their group photo which he found from Andria's room. 'What do you have to comment upon this?'

'Yeah, okay! I agree upon that. He is my cousin, but that doesn't mean I helped him out'. Surya realized she was not as vulnerable as he thought she was. She was clearly playing a game.

'What about the revolver, Beretta M9?' he pushed the revolver, wrapped in a polythene cover, toward Andria. 'I had seen it in your room the day before. The next day, I saw it in James's hand. How would it go to him without your help?'

'What's the proof that you had found it there?'

'I removed the bullets... I removed them that very day!' he said and showed the bullets in his hand. 'Do you really know that the Gun was empty?'

Surya confidently opened the magazine. It was full. Surya was shocked.

'Then why did you try to shoot me?'

'It was just an act of self-defense to protect my brother. I didn't even know what was going on then'.

'What about the CD you used to fake the death of James?' 'Do you remember what day it was?'

Surya checked out the calendar in his mobile. 'It was April 1st', he looked surprised. 'So, the CD was just a fake one to fool you.'

Surya had thought she would confess everything after being caught red–handed. Now, she had her own game to play.

He asked to turn off the camera and recorder. He turned out his pockets. 'Andria, why were you doing this?'

'What was I doing Surya? I am proving my innocence!'

'You are not innocent. You acted as Lydia and took Harshaja Gupta's number. This mobile is the proof. I know about Lydia! She was your cousin. Isn't this a plan to take revenge on Sudheer?' 'OH! So, you know all that! Why were you asking me then?'

'Tell me the truth, Andria. I know you are not that callous inside'.

'If you want the truth, it's not here', she whispered, getting closer to Surya, elevating her eyebrows. She stressed her voice, 'Take me to the woods!'

Surya leaned back in his chair, contemplating for a moment. Then he came out and asked Samar.

Samar asked, 'How are you going to trust her Surya? What if she escapes in the woods?' Surya affirmed, 'Give me a gun! I will shoot her if she tries to escape. We don't have any strong evidence against her'.

Samar thought for a while. 'Okay Surya! I will also come. You have no idea what could happen in the woods and I didn't find any worthy proof there. What if she hired some local bad guys to attack you?'

Surya contemplated and went into the interrogation room. He asked Andria about the coin of Samar. Within a second, she replied, 'Fine'.

They were headed toward Samar's jeep. Andria was there between them in handcuffs. Surya took the jeep keys from Samar who, in the meantime, took care of Andria by handcuffing her to the back of the jeep. They all headed toward the East Hill House. On the way, Samar asked, 'What about Kiran? Did you try to contact her? She could be our major witness'.

'Yeah, I tried contacting her. But she was out of coverage! Might be on some trek!' 'Yeah! Even I sent some of my men in search of her'.

They reached The East Hill House. Surya slowed down the jeep. He pushed the gate open and left the gate ajar. Samar unlocked the cuffs of Andria. She swung both her hands freely in the air with relief. All of them headed into the woods. 'Hey Surya! Why don't we go ahead of this Samar? He looks so moody'. Surya didn't understand how to respond to her. 'Seems like our chapter of live-in relationship is coming to an end'. They had rerouted the same course and finally reached at a spot in the woods where James called them previously. There was the turbulent sound of water hitting a surface as in waterfall. The woods ended with a cliff.

'Okay! Andria, tell us what you wanted to say?'

Andria took a leisurely walk for a minute to refresh herself. Then she gave a stern look. Her eyes welled up with tears. She wiped up trying to maintain her disposition, but still a teardrop trickled down her cheek which was defying the smile on her face.

'Do you know what Surya? Lydia was my cousin. We grew up together and we used to share everything. She was so sensitive. 1 and 15 months back it all happened. We were sharing the same room in the hostel, doing gaming course in Slovakia. James was my cousin. He was a drug addict. He needed money, for which he was dependent on Lydia. Lydia used to give him thinking he was spending for genuine reasons. Once she went to his apartment casually to give him a visit. She found him overdosed with Heroine. Immediately, she admitted him to a hospital and he underwent a rehab program. But there was an air of tension between them. She used to feel bad that she was the reason for all this. James finished his rehab program and re-entered his flat again. One day, he called Lydia asking for money! Lydia refused to give him as she was aware that he would spend that on drugs. He wanted easy money and was angry on Lydia. So one day, he casually went to her apartment. Lydia welcomed him as usual. When she was in the kitchen cooking food, he secretly arranged a camera in her bathroom and recorded her nude video. He sent the video to his friends in India to blackmail her for money. That guy did exactly what James wanted him to do. He started to blackmail her for a ransom of 1 million bucks in Indian currency in Goa, otherwise it would be leaked on the internet. She gave the money and got the video back. That's when Sudheer had copied her video and spread it among his friends. When she went to Slovakia, she realized what happened. She couldn't bear all that shame. Her father disowned her. Life became hard for her. I used to stay all the time with her to save her from doing anything she may regret. She assured me that she would be safe but just wanted some privacy. I went to get a tattoo in the remembrance of my Father. She went to the terrace of the building and called me. She told who were behind it – James and

Sudheer! And killed herself. Later, with the ashes of Lydia, I made this tattoo'. She showed her forearm from which she peeled off the fake skin. There were 3 heart-shaped tattoos with arrows piercing through it.

'My name is not Andria. I am Malia. I wanted to take revenge on them. I couldn't sleep at night as Lydia was always in my nightmares. When I saw her in the coffin, I developed a fear of closed places. When it gets dark, I see her as hallucination, which dreaded me a lot. I developed a fear for dark areas too. I developed control on my brain to overcome my fears and focus on my revenge. I couldn't forget her when she fell from the top of 10 floors. I wish I didn't leave her that time. So, I decided to take revenge on James and Sudheer. I did the groundwork on Sudheer and you while staying in Delhi. I got closer to you to take revenge on him. I lured James in, with a plan of blackmail. He was good at that thing, being experienced with Lydia. He readily accepted. I made him come here and planned. But Surya, I was giving hints to you to track him'.

ACP Samar and Surya looked dumbstruck. Surya said, 'I don't understand how to believe you after all this'.

'You don't need to believe me but believe your heart. Do you know what? That gun, Beretta M9, which you thought was unloaded, still had bullets. When I got a chance to kill you, I didn't! I took the loaded gun so that if anything goes wrong, I can kill James. I would never let you die', Surya was so confused.

Malia continued, 'But whatever happened between us was true! I was truly in love with you'. She welled up with tears. Surya felt his eyes becoming moist but controlled his emotions. 'I had to do this. Check your Facebook. Check what's viral now!'

Surya was shocked and checked immediately. He stood aghast. Sudheer's video of his affair with her boss' wife was viral on Facebook!

'I hope he got his punishment. James has to live the rest of his time in jail, but I think he deserves more'.

Samar got a phone call from his subordinates.

'What!' He looked aghast! He turned toward Surya, 'James has been found dead in our custody!'

Malia smiled. 'I mixed cyanide in his cigarettes.... Do you know why I asked you to come? Look at the tree'. Surya keenly looked at it. 'It has a small CCTV camera. The same which made me lose my best friend, which ruined my life, has to answer for everything'.

'Surya! I need you to telecast it in media. Everyone has to learn a lesson from it – how voyeurism and drugs cost your life' Surya felt awestruck with her. He felt proud for being in love with her.

All her memories flashed back, ending with a trickle of tears from his eyes. 'And only one person yet deserves punishment', Andria said.

Surya asked in shock, 'Who?'

'It's you Surya! I couldn't save my Lydia! You deserve this! I love you, Surya! But you let Sudheer make that video go viral. You need to know how it feels when someone close to you dies'. She showed her 3 tattoos and said, 'Do you know for whom and how I made this third "memorial tattoo"? I made it out of a little quantity of the blood you donated to Mary'. Surya was reminded of the victory tattoos of Mary, the kid who fought with cancer. 'I made the other tattoos for my father and Lydia, the only people I loved other than you'. Surya bent down on his knees. She apologetically went toward mountain cliff.

Surya was taken aback, 'What! No Malia! Don't do that. Please!' His eyes welled up with tears and he was running for her.

'Sorry, Surya!' Malia turned to the other side and dived from the cliff into the waterfalls. Surya was about to catch her but missed her and ended up by watching her body fall into the water which was 1000 feet below. It's impossible to survive that.

Surya couldn't believe what happened. He just kneeled down there ended up crying, shouting and freaking with anguish. All the memories of Malia, the first time he met her, the time they spent at the beach, the first kiss, the blood donation, the salsa all just flooded through his head.

He returned back to the East Hill House. All the local people were gathered there, police and forensic teams were coming out of the house. Surya went inside, taking slow strides, with his chest heaving. When he went inside, he saw Sudheer hanged to the ceiling in his bedroom. Surya looked aghast and suddenly went to catch the legs of Sudheer in a futile attempt to save him. Police moved the dead body to a mortuary in a van where James's dead body had also been kept. The bluish discoloration of his skin was obviously due to cyanide toxicity. The jailer who was the witness explained to Surya, 'He asked for a cigarette, sir. I just gave him one from his cigarette packet. He warmed the whole length of the cigarette before lighting it. After that, all of this happened'. Surya was reminded of his style of smoking.

EPILOGUE

Next day, Surya released the CCTV footage in the woods and telecast it. He did everything to promote in social media. It had become an overnight sensation. News channels were broadcasting the incident over and over again.... Everyone stuck to their television! Surya got an invitation, as he was also there in the video and did herculean efforts to promote the video, to speak before public. Surya spoke to the media in front of thousands of people over a stage.

'Malia, Lydia, Sudheer and James – who killed them? It's not that they killed each other. It was voyeurism, drug addiction and easy money that killed these people. It's time to learn our lesson. Our discipline should not end with simply muttering the Indian Pledge. We need to implement it. When a foreigner comes to our land out of respect, isn't it our responsibility to respect them? Women are the groundwork of this society. There is no nation without them. Is this the respect we are giving by leaking their bathroom videos, leaving them in severe agony and anguish? At least now you can realize the mistake and turn into better people, a better nation and a better world. It all starts with making a better 'you'. Focus on yourself. Bring Change within you! This nation will change automatically. Jai Hind!'

Everyone gave a standing ovation to Surya's speech. Surya was leaving the stage when the HOD, the CMO and Shravani came toward him. Shravani apologetically said, 'Sorry, sir! I misinterpreted your message and misunderstood you'.

The HOD grabbed his hand. 'Sorry from my side too', she said and smiled. His CMO wife was there too. She said, 'I am withdrawing the case, Surya. Sorry for troubling you'. Surya reciprocated with a gentle smile. 'Congrats, Surya!' Surya was confused why he was saying congrats. He wondered perhaps it was for having their daughter marry him. 'We cancelled DISCO... the disciplinary committee. So, you don't need to worry about that...'. Surya felt so happy for that. He said, 'Thank you so much, sir!' He was reminded of the dream he got before his Manali trek; the one in which he harassed the trio and laughed to himself. Somewhere in the corner, a woman with a scarf who listened to all his speech flickered a smile over her lips and dissolved in the gathering.

Surya too, while leaving the stage, flickered a smile on his face. He was reminded of the picture he saw in Lydia's album – a little girl wearing a swimming costume while handling a trophy.

While reaching his car, a familiar voice struck him. "Surya!" and young woman in Red clad walked gracefully towards him. Surya wheeled towards her halting from opening his car door. His eyes widened with warmth.

'I am sorry for your loss. My deep condolences for you' the woman, patted him.

'Thank you Raavi' Surya acknowledged her concern 'There is nothing much to do. It's their destiny'

The lawyer, Salsa dancer, experienced deep Scuba diver, multitalented woman nodded solemnly. But she looked lot younger than he saw her before. There were no wrinkles on her face. It appeared Manali had showered it's magic upon her or someway she found a mystical lake of eternal youth. Surya was about to ask her about this drastic change.

'Raavi Mam' A thin bespectacled man from the crowd with a well groomed hair a, wearing a formal suit, seems like the manager of the event, recognized her and reached her. 'What a sudden surprise?! You should have informed me in prior about your coming. I could have arranged your stay' the man said humbly. Surya kept staring him with an idiotic expression.

'How do you know her?'

'What are you saying, she is well known actress in Kollywood. It's surprising to hear that you don't know her!'

Surya incredulously gazed at her. Her sharp nose, dark penetrating eyes, well groomed silky hair, good physique with long legs and glistening red dress struck him with familiarity. 'The renowned actress, Ravali Mam?'

Raavi smirked 'Yes'

'You looked different then. Near you 30's though you lied you were around 50. Now you look you are in your 20s, I guess you are around 35'

'Thanks for your appraisal. Beauty is a god gift. Acting is just a natural flair for me. I entered this film industry with passion. Once, I entered inside, I realized its dark reality. Had to do lot of things which I didn't want to please the casting department to get opportunities. When I came to know about you though Malia, who I met in Salsa events in Manali, I was interested to meet you as you were also so frustrated about your profession. I disguised myself as an old lady to avoid any attention from public. In my vacation I visit those places to do the adventure activities I want to do as a normal woman without popularity. I love living that way.'

'That's so nice about you. As all people are craving for popularity, you want to live like yourself' His eyes brightened with appreciation 'You are a real inspiration'

'Don't flatter much.' Raavi winked. 'I never thought Malia had those hidden intentions. I don't judge her. If I were in her position, I would have done the same' She puffed a deep sigh with her face contorted to a melancholic look. 'In my young age even I went through a lot of suffering. My father used my Mom and left her when he got an opportunity to marry another woman whose father promised him with better future and wealth. My mother was pregnant then and I was a teenage girl. He used to send us some money initially through we survived somehow. Later he stopped sending that. We struggled a lot to go through our basic needs. Then I got the opportunity as an artist in a drama company looking at my skills. I was 16 then. Slowly, my journey as an artist began. I got more opportunities in Kollywood so I shifted there'

'Thank heavens. Quite story it is. It is how someone's life should be. Full of drama and twists. Don't say you too have a revenge story. If you want to have one, tell me before I turn into a pawn in your story too. My life is quite boring'

'Well, Malia changed your life now. I don't think your life would be same way anymore.' She laughed. 'I wanted to ask you. Why are you stressed with your life?'

Surya paused for a moment to take deep breath and said with a grimace in his face. 'I had a love failure before this trip. I didn't share it to anyone in the trip including Malia. Her Name is Fathima. My intern. One day there was a terrible attack on Doctors in our Hospital. After recovering, I didn't see her again. Some said she exiled with her father who was undercover cop for a longtime. These girls are so enigmatic creatures. I was all for her before her father and now he became everything and left me unnoticed.' He said sulking. Raavi gave a concerned look. 'Now, Malia also betrayed me. Whoever I love, just leave me alone' he pretended a laugh with overwhelming sadness still lurking behind his eyes.

'I am sorry. I know how you feel now.' She flickered a gentle smile on her lips. 'I understand your loss.' Her phone rang. 'Excuse me' She went aside and talked discreetly

Later she approached him with a regretting expression 'I have a shooting here nearby. I will catch you later' She gave him a warm hug. 'Take care. Call me whenever you needed. Consider me as your sister'. She gave hers visiting card. He smiled and reverted back to his Car and stepped inside.

'I will write a book on this experience, he shouted looking from the window of car at Raavi who looked over her shoulder and shouted with an exuberant face 'Good luck with that' She cheered him up and turned away with a smile which slowly contorted to a grim look. She took a red color car parked nearby and drove away swiftly.